PERSONAL

ST. LOUIS CYCLONES: BOOK 3

ALEXANDRIA HOUSE

COPYRIGHT

EPIGRAPH

"The true measure of a man is not how he behaves in moments of comfort and convenience but how he stands at times of controversy and challenges." — Martin Luther King Jr.

"The most common way people give up their power is by thinking they don't have any."
— Alice Walker

PROLOGUE

ARMAND

He's coming up on the left, pivot right, dribble, fake a pass, eyes on the goal, gotta get the ball there, but this nigga is ***on me*** *on me.*

"Daniels!" That was Brickey letting me know he was open, but I couldn't shake the big motherfucker who was guarding me.

Shit.

Sweat rolled down my face as I dribbled, moving left—then right—then left at top speed, managing to make my opponent stumble a little but enough to give me an opening, I let the ball go, watching as it sailed through the air...and missed the damn hoop.

Mother. Fuck.

The buzzer sounded signaling the beginning of halftime, and I couldn't wait to get to the locker room and away from the rude-ass fans I knew would be talking shit as we left the court. I was good as long as they didn't throw nothing at me because I didn't mind climbing the bleachers and fucking someone up. Yeah, we were down by ten points, but that shit couldn't be blamed on me just because of this one missed shot. At least there was a *chance* I could've made it. Brickey's ass was almost guaranteed to miss.

I kept my eyes ahead of me, moving into the tunnel with jeers from fans filling my ears.

Fuck them.

Fuck *all* of them.

It amazed me how a bunch of folks who couldn't dribble a ball let alone run up and down a court like we did night after night passed judgement on our performances. Out of shape, miserable, no talent having, fickle assholes—that's what they were.

Once I made it to the locker room, I headed to my locker and my phone, ignoring the looks my teammates were shooting at me and only half-listening to the coach go over the highlights, or really, the *lowlights*, of the first half of the game. A locker room attendant handed me a water bottle full of what I knew to be a drink suffused with electrolytes, a specialized blend a member of the team's dietary crew prescribed for me since I was known to sweat more than most. I was quickly navigating to Twitter to see if my fuckup was a trending topic when I felt someone standing over me. Raising my eyes, I stared at the attendant who usually would've handed me my drink and disappeared. He looked...concerned, but I had no idea why. I stared back at him for a moment, and I guess that was enough to make him leave because he did. Shaking my head, I refocused on my phone and the Twitter app to see that I *was* a trending topic.

I sighed, glancing up long enough to see that more eyes were on me.

What the fuck?

Yeah, I missed the shot, but got damn! Everyone missed a shot from time to time, even Drayveon Walker!

I closed my eyes and told myself I couldn't start fucking my teammates up. I'd promised Nathan Moore, my agent who was really more than my agent, that I would act like I had some sense and stop fighting people. But this shit was just strange. To avoid doing some shit that whoever I did it to would regret, I went against my first mind and actually looked at some of the tweets that mentioned me, my eyes narrowing and my heart rate accelerating with each post I read.

I know damn well I'm not seeing what I'm seeing. This shit can't be true.

I kept scrolling and reading and scrolling and reading until I could feel my temple pulsing, my knee started bouncing, and heat began crawling up my neck to my face.

These motherfuckers...

"Daniels!"

My head snapped up to see the locker room emptying and Coach standing over me. I didn't respond to him because I couldn't.

I fucking couldn't.

"You heard?" he asked, his voice its usual low rumble, his face bearing its standard impassive expression. I suppose he knew there was no need to elaborate.

Still, I didn't, *couldn't* respond.

Coach shook his head and sighed before turning to leave but stopped in his tracks when I said, "So everybody knew but me?"

Glancing at me over his shoulder, he shook his head again. "No. I knew it was in the works, but I didn't find out the trade had been finalized until during the game. Look, you're talented and I like you, but the owners see you as a liability."

"A what?!" I yelled.

"A *liability*. You're too...unpredictable, volatile. Listen, the best thing you can do right now is get back out on that court and make this last Pistons game your best."

I had a lot of respect for Coach, a black man who understood me. At least I *believed* he did. Turns out he didn't, but that wasn't surprising. No one understood me. Rarely did anyone even try.

"Nah, y'all got it. If I'm out, I'm out. I ain't playing no got damn second half," I bit out.

He sighed as he exited the locker room. "Well, Daniels...that's a damn disappointment."

And that? That's when I blacked the fuck out.

ONE

ARMAND

Sportscaster one: "The biggest news coming from the NBA this week is the mid-game Armand Daniels trade from the Pistons to the Cyclones."

Sportscaster two: "Yes, Dave, and although Stevie Wonder probably saw this trade coming, it's been reported that Armand Daniels' reaction to the news was, in one word, explosive."

Sportscaster one: "Well, Bill...I'm not sure ***reported*** *is the best word since there's recorded footage of his reaction. Let's take a look."*

The scene on the screen shifted from inside the Black Sports Network studio to the Pistons' locker room. The blue carpet with the centered Pistons logo coming into view first, then me sitting in the chair at my locker, my eyes focused on the room's entrance. Whoever filmed me zoomed in on my face, and the expression on it actually scared me. I was pissed, like *pissed* pissed. Just watching myself brought back feelings that still pulled at my sanity. This video captured me moments after Coach called me a fucking disappointment and chronicled a pocket of time I honestly had no recollection of. But there I was, plain as damn day, standing from my chair, throwing my phone first, then my chair, then other chairs, making them hit the wall under the screen, which at that moment, was showing the second half of the game. While I wrecked shit, I could be heard yelling all kinds of stuff like, "Fuck this team!"

Or "These motherfuckers can kiss my ass!"

Or "A disappointment?! Fuck him!"

It was uncomfortable to watch, but I didn't feel bad for doing it. I was tired of being traded. I couldn't lay down any roots like this. I couldn't find any equilibrium. I couldn't build anything. I just wanted some got damn stability.

The video ended, and just as Bill's and Dave's bitch-ass faces reappeared on the screen, Nathan Moore reached for the remote, turning the TV off. The room fell silent until I finally looked over at him sitting in a chair in my living room in my temporary-ass apartment in this temporary-ass city.

"Go ahead," I muttered, "say what you flew all the way here from Tennessee to say. Say you told me this was coming, that I shouldn't have been shocked, that I racked up a fine for tearing up that locker room for nothing, that I'm lucky they didn't have me arrested instead of just having security drag my ass off the premises."

He leaned back in the chair, straightening his tie before lifting his hands. "You've said it all, which begs the question: *what the fuck is wrong with you*?" His response came with thunder in his voice. Shit, he almost startled me.

Almost, but I ain't no punk, so...

"Ain't nothing wrong with me," I shot back, leaning forward on my sofa and shaking my head. "You can't see how fucked up it is for me to keep getting traded?! Miami, New Orleans...hell, this is my second go with Detroit! These motherfuckers are trading me for a second time! And now the Cyclones? The fucking Cyclones?!"

"The Cyclones are a good team. Your volatile ass is lucky they want you."

Waving my hand, I said, "Yeah, yeah, whatever. I'm one of the best players in the league. I know it. You know it. The Cyclones know it. They ain't doing me no got damn favors."

"Yeah, they are! Look, Armand...you're talented. *You are.* I've said this tons of times before, but I'll say it again—you have the potential to be one of the greats if you don't fuck your own chances up. You're unlikeable, unstable, and uncooperative as hell. All these years in the league and you're still a ball hog?"

"I miss one damn shot and—"

"It ain't about that! You don't know how to be a teammate! You don't know how to have anyone's back but your own, and you aren't exactly doing a good job of that. To be honest, I'm tired of your shit."

"Man, fuck you! You don't wanna represent me anymore, then step. I don't need you. I don't need nobody!"

"Here you go with that you against the world shit. The only person doing you wrong is *you*."

I was done talking because this was the same shit he always said when trouble hit. Wasn't nothing for me to say, so we both just sat there for like ten minutes. Finally, I asked, "You quitting?"

"You for real this time? You want me to quit?"

"I don't wanna be on no damn team with Leland McClain. We cool but not *that* cool," I said, ignoring his question.

"Well, I can look into some overseas teams, or maybe you wanna go semi-pro."

I looked up to see him wearing a smirk.

In response, I grinned and shook my head at this man who'd been putting up with my shit longer than most ever would, and said, "Man, fuck you, Nate," making him laugh.

"The first thing you're going to do when you get to St. Louis is find a therapist. No more bullshit about you not having enough time and no more quitting after one or two visits. This is a deal breaker for me. If you don't resume therapy, I'm going to drop your ass as a client *for real*, Daniels."

I stared at him before reclining on the sofa and blowing out a breath. "I hear you."

ELLA

I hugged my stepmom, Jo, and my siblings, Nat, Lena, Lil' Ev, and the twins, Ever and Jonah, blinking back tears as I watched them file out of the house—one twin on Jo's hip and one on Nat's although they were both toddlers, *rambunctious* toddlers. Then it was just me and the big guy.

He'd been leaning against the foyer wall watching me say my goodbyes. Now, he was approaching me, a heavy sadness clouding his face as he took mine into his big hands.

"You can come visit whenever you want. You can call me anytime, day or night," he said.

"I know, Daddy," I replied, still fighting tears.

"You don't go anywhere without security. *Anywhere.*"

"Daddy, I am twenty-three years old. I've lived separate from you before. I went to college; then I stayed in New York for a whole year. I'll be fine."

Ignoring my statement, he continued with, "You didn't have to move, Princess. I wouldn't have been in your business. I know you're grown and deserve your privacy."

"I appreciate that, but I...I just needed a change. I'll be okay, I promise, and if at any moment I don't feel okay, I'll let you know. Plus, I have Mother Erica on speed dial, and Uncle Leland is just thirty minutes away. Remember? You insisted that if I moved out of LA, I had to still be near a relative, just like in college."

My daddy, *the* Big South, nodded before planting a soft kiss on my forehead and pulling me into a tight hug. Leaning into the protection and comfort I'd always felt flowing from him to me, I shut my eyes tightly and inhaled his scent. I loved my father more than anyone else in the world, and if I was honest with myself, I'd have to admit that I didn't want to leave him or the rest of my nuclear family, but I knew I needed to. I needed to prove to myself that I could stand on my own two feet, that I could cope and thrive without the umbrella of sanctuary my dad willingly and enthusiastically held over me.

When he finally released me, I saw that his eyes were wet. Giving him my bravest smile, I reached up, pulling his head down so that I could kiss his forehead. "You'll be okay," I said.

He chuckled before kissing my cheek and exiting through my front door. I stood there watching as their SUV left my driveway, shut the door to my new home, and then collapsed into tears.

TWO

ELLA

"Mon ange! I've been awaiting your call! You are in Missouri, I trust? Your papa has, uh...tucked you in?"

I giggled at hearing his voice, his French accent thick and curvy. "Tucked me in? I'm not a child, Claude."

He sucked his tongue. "You know what I mean. He bought you a house, no? So, you are uh...squared away?"

"I am. You know my dad, always going above and beyond. Three bedrooms, four bathrooms, three thousand square feet of luxury fully furnished, and all this for little old me."

"Everett McClain is a good man, mon ange. Always has been. He loves you as a father should."

"I know. I'm a lucky girl in many ways. So, how are you? Taking your meds? Staying away from the liquor?"

"You nag!" Claude DuMont groaned. For a man in his sixties, he could be downright pigheaded about taking care of himself. "You might be my favorite model, but that doesn't mean I want to hear your fussing. I'm fine! Hans makes sure of that. And here he is now with a smoothie or something. It's green. You know I hate the color green." Hans was his main lover of many years, but Claude had a trail of broken male and female hearts cluttering his past.

"I do know that. Tell Hans I said hi. You drink your smoothie, and I'll call you later."

"All right, mon ange. Call your mother, chérie."

Before I could reply, he hung up and I sighed, resting against the back of the sofa in my new living room. I loved Claude DuMont, a legendary designer who'd taken me under his wing from the very beginning of my modeling career. He was a dear friend, a mentor, and there wasn't much I'd ever refused him, but I wasn't calling my mother.

Not today.

Not ever, if I could help it.

Feeling that way killed the good vibes chatting with Claude always gave me, but I was sadly accustomed to my emotions being in a pit anyway. Loss could do that to you. Loss, pain, despair—I was uncomfortably familiar with those states of being. I'd spent a lot of time dwelling in darkness, so much so that being in the light felt...foreign. Nevertheless, I'd continue to fight to keep the void behind me. I'd almost lost myself before. I couldn't let that happen again.

ARMAND

She a baddie and she mine
Prime rib, perfection defined
Long legs, a pretty face
All eyes on her when she steps in the place...

On One's *Mine* blasted from the speakers of my Urus as I rode through the streets of my hometown, checking out neighborhoods mainly on the north side where my mom and I lived while I was growing up. Every time I came home, it seemed shit just got worse and worse. A lot of my old friends were either dead, in jail, running from the law, or had left the city altogether, but there were a few who were still here and had managed to upgrade. My boy, Scotty, was one of those few, and being able to hang with him on the regular was one of the scarce positives about this move. That, and I'd be close to family—my granny, my cousins, aunts, and uncles, my mom.

My mom.

If "it's complicated" could apply to mother/son relationships, it'd fit us like a glove. There wasn't a person on this rock that I loved more. There also wasn't a person on this rock who'd hurt me more.

See? Complicated.

On One continued to provide the soundtrack for my ride through Da Lou as my mind wandered. Dude had a weird voice when he rapped, a cross between DMX and Pac. Like, he was smooth and gritty at the same time, God rest his soul. Ain't no way On One should've died so young, but life for a black man was nothing if not perilous. We never knew when the dagger hanging over our heads would fall. Wasn't no hiding from that shit.

I was heading back to my hotel when she called. My first thought was to ignore it. My second thought was to ignore it, too. My third thought was to answer, but I was too late, so I called her back.

She answered with, "Hey, Boogie. You in town?" She sounded excited as hell. I wished I felt the same.

Pulling to a stop at a red light, I shut my eyes for a second before replying, "Yes, ma'am."

"Good! Where are you staying?"

"Uh...I got a room at the Sable Inn for now."

"Oh..." I knew she wanted me to stay in the little cottage on her and her husband's property, but bump that.

"Yeah. Ma, I gotta go. In traffic."

"Oh, okay. Well, I'm glad you're here. Hope to see you soon."

"Yeah," I said, and then I hung up.

MY BOY since forever smacked my shoulder. "Man, I'm glad you're in town! How's it feel to be back home?"

I shrugged, taking a seat at the bar in his kitchen. "Weird as fuck, familiar and unfamiliar at the same time."

Scotty nodded, his back to me now as he worked at the stove in his downtown loft. Dude had a nice crib, exposed brick and pipes, sleek furniture. I suppose being a business owner was working out for him, and his clothing line for big and tall men was dope as hell. "I hear you," he replied. "A lot of shit has changed but a lot of shit is the same."

"Yeah. When you learn how to cook?"

He glanced over his beefy shoulder, giving me a smirk. "I *been* knowing how to cook, nigga. I'm big, gotta know how to cook."

"You ain't never cook nothing for me before."

"I ain't fucking you, fool."

I laughed. "Damn, okay. So your girl got you like that? You clean and do laundry, too?"

"Cook, clean, do laundry, eat pussy. Shiiiid, I'll tap dance for that pussy. You just don't know!"

I fell out laughing. "Nigga, you sprung?!"

"I'm in this motherfucker going boing-boing, my guy!"

We both laughed.

Shaking my head, I said, "I can't believe this. Next thing I know, your ass gon' be married with kids."

"That's the plan."

My eyes damn near popped out of my head. "Scotty, you for real?!" I could party, but this dude was the partying final boss.

"*For real*. Man, we hittin' our thirties. I found a good woman and I ain't got time to fuck it up. I'm keeping my ass out the clubs and out of chicks' DMs. This thing me and Rory got? This some forever shit."

"So...wait, I finally get on the home team and your ass ain't gon' kick it with me?"

"Hell naw I ain't!"

"That's fucked up, Burgess!"

"I don't care about you using my first name. I *still* ain't going to no clubs with you. Dinwiddie still in the streets. Lance, too. They got you."

"Ain't Dinwiddie married now?"

"Supposedly. He don't act like it though."

"I'd probably be the same way. Ain't no female finna tame me. Believe that shit."

"Nah, I thought the same thing, but the right woman will have you rolling over and playing dead for that ass. Hell, Rory got me aligning my chakras and recycling plastics."

I gave him a smirk. "Nah, I ain't letting that happen to me. I am *not* going out like that."

"Wanna bet?"

"Bet!"

"How much we talking, 'cause that's a bet I'll take."

"A hunnid."

"A'ight, my guy. It's on!"

THREE

ARMAND

I hated this shit.

I really, *really* hated this shit, the awkward phase of joining a new team with established chemistry, that new guy feeling. That odd man out crap. I fucking despised it, and I'm sure my face revealed my extreme animosity the second I stepped onto the Cyclones practice court. When I saw my stepfather, who was one of the senior members of the team, I'm not ashamed to admit I wanted to break and run. Leland McClain made me confront issues I didn't ever want to face.

What made things worse was how nice everyone was. Nice, inviting, downright hospitable.

What the fuck?

Didn't they know who I was, *what* I was? Didn't they know I'd beat the shit out of any one of them if they pissed me off? Didn't they know I operated on a hair trigger? Were they too dumb to see I wasn't nobody's friend? Well, nobody but Burgess Scott Smith,

Jr. Damn, not only was I on a new team, but a new team of dummies.

The coach, though? Now, he was my speed. He was a yelling, screaming, asshole. I could vibe with him.

"All right, motherfuckers! Gather 'round. Wait, where the fuck is Walker?" Coach Duke thundered. He was tall *and* wide, a dark-skinned man in a white Cyclones polo shirt and khaki pants. He kind of reminded me of that dude from that one show—*The Unit*.

"He had to hit the bathroom, Coach," Polo Logan said. I didn't know Polo personally, but of course I knew him when I saw him.

"He stays his ass in the bathroom. I thought his wife was pregnant, not him! The fuck he acting like he got a baby sitting on his bladder for?!" Coach Duke yelled. Damn, did this dude ever *not* yell? Shit!

"Here he comes. Youngin', bring your ass on!" That was my mother's husband. I made sure to keep my eyes off him. Like I said before, we were straight, but that was only because he was good to my mom. We weren't *ever* going to be buddies.

Never damn ever.

"All right, now that you're all here, let me introduce you to your new teammate, Armand Daniels! He's related to McClain, as most of you know, and he's talented as hell!" the coach announced, and yes, he was *still* yelling.

I lifted my eyes from the shiny court floor to watch as the group of players nodded and greeted me. In return, I gave them a halfhearted, "'Sup."

"Daniels, I want you to follow me. The rest of y'all know what to do. Isom, you got it today," Coach Duke boomed, handing practice over to his assistant. A moment later, I was following him off the practice court through the Cyclones complex to his huge office and taking the seat he offered me in front of his desk.

"Just a moment," he said, answering the phone on his desk that was already ringing as we entered the office. I had no idea why he needed to see me privately. I'd already endured conference calls with Nate and the general manager. I knew what was expected of me; it wasn't like this was my first rodeo when it came to organizations, new coaches, new everything. I also knew while I was guaranteed to meet those expectations on the court, it wouldn't be enough.

It never was.

I tuned whatever conversation he was having out as I let my eyes tour his office. It was par for the course as far as those types of office spaces went—expensive furniture, diplomas on the walls, trophy cases, championship rings on display. Same old same old. Coach Marteese Duke was a legendary college basketball coach before taking the helm for the Cyclones. Before that, he was once an NBA legend, a notable point guard for the Celtics. He was a man who commanded respect, and I liked him for his gruffness if nothing else. I really hoped he wasn't about to say some shit that would piss me off.

"Sorry about that, Daniels," he said, pulling my attention from the white walls and dark furniture to him.

"No problem. Uh...is there some paperwork I need to fill out or something? I thought I handled all that already," I replied.

"No. No paperwork. I wanted to give you the information I promised Nate Moore I'd pass on to you."

"Oh...what info?" I asked, frowning.

He lifted a piece of paper from his desk and held it up. "Your appointment confirmation."

"Appointment confirmation? What? I need another physical or something? A drug test? Already done."

"No. Your therapy appointment."

As I sat up straight in my chair, my frown deepened. "Therapist? I didn't make a therapy appointment. I mean...I'm going to, but I ain't made one yet. I ain't had the chance."

Coach Duke nodded. "Nate figured as much, so he called and asked that we handle it for you. The therapist's name is Alvin Charles. He's a friend to the organization and has worked with a lot of the players and staff in the past. He's taking you on as a special favor to the GM."

"I...what? Y'all can't make me see some dude I don't know," I said, fighting hard not to go completely off. "I ain't y'all's slave!"

"No, you're not. You're a Cyclones Organization employee. You're also a young man a good friend of mine believes in. I've known Nathan Moore for years. So have the owners. He's the only reason you're here, him and his promise that you'd work on that temper of yours that's flaring up right now. The therapist is a deal-breaker, Daniels."

I stared at this man, clenching my fists as they rested on the arm of the chair. I didn't respond verbally, and it took everything in me not to climb over that desk and fuck this man up. Then I felt it, that familiar sense of time slipping out of my hands, of everything around me fading, until I heard, "Armand."

My eyes snapped up from where they'd wandered to the floor without me realizing it, landing on the phone sitting atop Duke's desk. Was that Nathan Moore's voice I heard, or was I hearing shit?

"Armand," he repeated. It *was* Nathan.

"Huh?" I said, feeling disoriented as hell. Then I redirected my attention to Duke. "You called him or something?"

He nodded, moving the phone closer to me.

"Coach Duke, can you give us a moment alone?" Nate asked.

"Sure thing," Coach said, his voice calmer than it had been all day.

I heard rather than saw Coach leave the office as the door shut behind him, and then I just stared at the phone.

"Armand, you still there?" Nathan asked.

"I didn't do nothing," was how I chose to answer him.

"I know. Your first appointment is in a couple of days. Don't miss it."

"Nate—"

"*Don't miss it*, and calm your ass down before you go back out on that court unless you're ready to be benched for good."

I unclenched my hands and sighed before finally saying, "Yeah."

ELLA

"Hi, darling. It's been a while since we've chatted. Just wanted to hear your voice and see how things are going in St. Louis. I heard you're walking for House of DuMont during Fashion Week in Paris. I hate I had to get the news secondhand. Ella...I just...I miss you. Call me back, okay?"

I pulled the phone from my ear after my mother's message ended, finding myself staring at nothing as I lay in my bed, what seemed to be my favorite spot in this big house. That was probably because I could sleep now, and I was so happy about it that I didn't want to leave the location of this new miracle. A year ago, sleep was a distant memory and a deep desire all rolled into one big ball of despair. Life was still hard for me, but I'd come far.

Very far.

I'd handed my social media accounts over to a professional the day I checked into the Sankofa Healing Center, and I honestly believe that decision had fueled my recovery. A couple of months ago, I decided to reclaim control of my Instagram account, and as I navigated to the app, I braced myself for what I was sure I would and did find—tag after tag on posts paying tribute, fan art, inspirational quotes. Sighing, I closed the app and my eyes. I didn't want to think about that part of my life anymore. I didn't want to have to keep reliving that stuff.

I just wanted to move on.

. . .

THE CHIMING of my phone awakened me from a sleep I'd unconsciously drifted into, causing my heart to jump. Grabbing my phone from the bed, I saw the preview of a text message from my Uncle Leland and smiled. I'd been in town for two weeks and hadn't even called him. I guessed my time was up.

Dinner at my house next Thursday. Seven o'clock. Bring a date if you want to, if you find one who's brave enough to face me. Can't wait to see you, baby girl.

Still smiling, I replied: *I can't wait to see you either.*

Then I dialed my best friend's number.

FOUR

ARMAND

"How's practice been going?" she asked, the familiarity of her gravelly voice making me smile.

"It's been cool, I guess," I said.

"You guess? You're back home—although you haven't been over to see me—you're around family, you're on the same team as that sweet, sweet Leland. You should be sounding happier than this!"

Man, ever since she joined the Leland McClain fan club, my grandmother had been hard as hell for me to talk to. Like right now? All I could do was hold the phone because what?

"Boogie, I know you were angry about him and your mother before, but we talked about this. We've talked about it many times. Your mother doesn't always make the best decisions, but I thought we both agreed that Leland is good for her. Good *to* her, too!"

"I know all that, Grandma. It's just...I don't know."

"And those babies! You gotta love the babies!"

I shrugged as if she could see me. "I'ont know them, Grandma."

"Well, you should!"

Silence from me.

"Oh! Your uncle Kent is calling me! I'll talk to you later, Boogie!"

Thank God. "A'ight, Grandma."

I was glad as a motherfucker for that save.

Placing my phone in my locker, I pulled a t-shirt over my head as teammates passed in and out of the room. So far, they'd been leaving me alone, and I appreciated it. That was all I ever really wanted anyway. I didn't like most people, and the ones I liked, I could only take in small doses.

"Aye, Daniels. Can I talk to you for a minute?"

I shut my eyes and dropped my shoulders. So much for being left alone. "McClain, man. Look—"

"Daniels, come on...I thought we were cool or at least semi-cool. I ain't proved to you that I got your mom's best interest at heart by now?"

I looked up at my mom's husband, a nigga who was literally only seven years older than me and young enough to still be playing in the league, a dude who was once my teammate, and shook my head. "We ain't never gon' be cool, but I can tolerate you if you keep doing what you been doing—leaving me the fuck alone."

He sighed, grasping the towel around his neck. I was glad he had a shirt and shorts on. I wasn't trying to see that big-ass tattoo he had of my mom's name on his chest. "Look, your mom wanted me to invite you to dinner next week at our place. She said she'll text you the details because she knows you don't like to talk on the phone."

Before I could tell him, "*Hell no*," he turned and walked away.

I quickly dressed and left.

. . .

I WAS FEELING PRETTY GOOD. I'd balled my ass off during my first home game, and I have to admit that this team was probably one of the most harmonious ones I'd ever been a part of. These dudes were cool both on and off the court and talented as hell. Drayveon Walker? That nigga was a beast with the ball. There weren't many who could get the ball through the hoop like him with the exception of Steph Curry. I mean, I wasn't one to be a fan of other players, but I was actually kind of honored to be sharing the court with Walker.

My good mood was overshadowed by the fact that the very next day, I found myself sitting in a waiting room filling out paperwork. It was the day of my first therapy appointment in a long-ass time, something I'd been avoiding like the plague because who in their right mind wanted to sit up and discuss their own insanity? Did I know I was crazy? Hell-yeah! Did I want to talk about it, face it, shit, even contemplate it?

Hell-no!

Nevertheless, these folks—the Cyclones, my agent—were forcing me into this shit because contrary to what many folks might think, I loved my job. I loved playing in the league. Being good at basketball was the only thing I had, and I was at the top. You can't go further than the NBA. I damn sure wasn't trying to go down to the semi-pros. So, I was doing this, although I knew it wasn't going to make a difference. I'd tried more than once in the past and it never worked out. I wouldn't vibe with the therapist, or they'd annoy me by asking silly-ass questions, or—

"Mr. Daniels?"

My head snapped up from the clipboard I was holding to the face of the receptionist behind the open sliding glass window. "Yes?" I replied.

"Mr. Charles will see you now. I'll take your paperwork if you're done."

I stood from my seat and nodded, first taking the few steps to give her the clipboard and pen, and then turning and facing the door to the therapist's inner office. I stood there for damn near a whole minute before slowly making my way to that door and opening it.

The inner office was like a smaller version of the waiting room. Same colors, lots of potted plants. No desk, just a nice leather chair and a loveseat that was probably too short for me. Mr. Charles was sitting in the chair, his eyes on me as if he was sizing me up or something. So I stared right back at his ass.

Finally, he glanced at his watch and said, "Mr. Daniels...have a seat," in a midrange voice—not exactly deep but not shrill either.

I nodded, plopped down on the loveseat, and was glad my knees weren't touching my damn chest.

I'd stretched my legs out and was getting comfortable when he went right in with the bullshit, saying, "I'm sure you know I'm Alvin Charles and I know why *I'm* here. Tell me why *you're* here."

I had to fight not to roll my eyes. "Obviously, I'm not here to play spades."

"I didn't say you were, and that doesn't answer the question, Mr. Daniels."

So this nigga was getting smart, huh? "A'ight. I'm here because everybody seems to think I'm fucked up in the head."

"Okay, who is everybody?"

"Everybody is *everybody*. If you don't know what the word means, look it up," I replied, straightening in my seat. Dude was already getting on my fucking nerves.

"Oh, I know what the word means. So, you're including yourself in that? Do you think you're fucked up in the head?"

I shrugged. "I don't know. I am who I am. Ain't my fault people be pissing me off."

"People as in everybody?"

"Yep."

"How does everybody piss you off?"

I stared at him for a long moment before shaking my head. "I... can we end this right now? I can't. I'ont like how this feels. Can you just tell the folks at my team that I came and we talked so I can be done with this shit?"

"I can do that, but as I understand it, they're *requiring* you to attend weekly therapy sessions."

"Yeah, I know that, but I..."

The room fell silent. I couldn't verbalize what I was feeling in a way that wouldn't have dude ready to recommend me for an inpatient stay in a psych ward. Talking about myself, my feelings, the stuff that bothered me? It made me feel like my skin was on my body too tight, like my head was on my neck backwards or some shit. It was the most uncomfortable state of being for me, made me want to crawl out of myself.

In the quietude, I kept my eyes on the window behind Mr. Charles but could feel his eyes on me. I'm not sure how many minutes passed like that, and I don't know why I didn't just get up and leave.

When I knew anything, he was clearing his throat, and then he spoke. "Mr. Daniels, your next appointment is on next Friday. Same time."

As he stood and opened the door for me, I lifted from the loveseat and shook my head. "Look," I said, "I'm not—"

"I trust that you completed the required paperwork, so we should have your email on file. I'm going to send you some information. Have a good rest of your day," he interrupted me, and before I could say a word, he'd called another patient's name, officially dismissing me.

FIVE

ELLA

"How and where'd you find a professional makeup artist in St. Louis so fast? You've only been here for a few weeks!" my bestie observed.

"Oh, I scoped that out before I left LA. You know that's what I did when I moved to New York," I replied, "since my uncle won't let me steal my Aunt Sage from him."

"Riiiiiiiggght, Miss Supreme Diva! You don't play about your appearance!"

"Act like you know, negro!"

He stared at me before we both burst into laughter. I was so glad he was in St. Louis that I felt giddy.

"Well, she got you right. Looking good, baby. Real good," he said.

"Awww, thanks, Carlos. You flirting with me?"

"Hell no! I know all your secrets, which means I'm privy to just how crazy you are. I'll pass."

I held my middle finger up at him, making him laugh again.

"But real talk, I'm proud of you, Ella J. I know how hard things have been for you, what you've been through. I know how far you've come."

I gave him a faint smile as I stared at his reflection in my vanity mirror. Carlos Vera was big and tall, a former football player who appeared intimidating, but as I knew, was a super good guy, the son of Afro-Cuban immigrants who left football behind after we both graduated from TSU, subsequently joining me in the world of modeling. While I'd backed away from my career, only accepting a handful of gigs after life dealt me successive blows, Carlos was still taking full advantage of every opportunity that presented itself to him. It was no small thing that he'd made time to fly from NYC to St. Louis just to have dinner with me at my uncle's house, but he understood me and my quirks, the ones I'd developed in an attempt to lead a pseudo-normal life. I mean, at least I was *going* to my uncle's house. There was a period of time when my only view was the four walls of my bedroom at my dad's place.

Yeah, I'd definitely made progress.

"Maybe I should wear a wig," I mumbled more to myself.

Carlos shook his head where he was seated behind me on the foot of my bed. "Don't start..."

I rolled my eyes, adjusting my butt on the vanity bench. "I'm just saying...I like my wigs," I elaborated.

"How do you even manage to shove all that hair under a wig? Seems like a lot of useless work."

I dragged the fingers of my right hand through the bone straight strands of my recently silk-pressed hair and sighed. "I don't know. I guess I just need a change. I'm tired of looking like this."

"What? Beautiful? You're tired of looking beautiful?"

"I'm tired of looking so much like Esther Reese, actually."

"Shiiit, your mom's one of the baddest chicks to ever chick!

Ain't a damn thing wrong with looking like Esther 'still fine as fuck' Reese. You trippin'!"

I turned in my seat and lifted an eyebrow as I glared at him.

Raising his hands, he said, "Are her morals questionable? Yes. Do I get why you don't like her? Absolutely, but we ain't gonna sit here and pretend like your mom ain't *that bitch*."

"Get out so I can get dressed," I said flatly.

"Why I gotta leave? Ain't like I've never seen you naked, baby."

"And we are both in agreement that that was a major mistake. Get out, Carlos Nestor Vera! Now!"

"Okay, okay. Hurry up. I'm ready to eat!" he shouted over his shoulder as he left my bedroom.

Standing from the vanity and letting my toes sink into the plush pink rug covering the hardwood floor, I took the few steps to my closet, quickly pulled on my white Gucci crop tee, a pair of faded Balenciaga skinny jeans, a green Gucci blazer, and a bad-ass pair of black NeroGiardini boots. Giving myself a once over in the mirrored door of my closet, I sighed. I looked good as hell, but inside, I still felt a hollowness I just couldn't seem to shake.

Yes, I'd come a long way, but I still had a way to go.

ARMAND

Sorry, Ma. I'm not gonna make it to dinner.

I hit send on the text to my mother and fell into the bed in my suite. I'd been in St. Louis for a couple weeks and hadn't even attempted to find me a place mostly because I wasn't sure how permanent this move would be for me. I'd also opted out of staying with my grandma or any other relative because I didn't need or want them all up in my business, and my mother? I wasn't concerned about her being in my business; I just...couldn't. I couldn't stay at her place even if she did have a whole separate house set up for me. Wasn't no way I could. So, I was still spending way too much money on a fancy-ass suite.

We didn't have a game that night, which was probably why my mom chose it for the dinner. On off nights, I usually hit the streets to see what I could get into. I'm not sure why I decided to stay in staring at my phone instead, perusing Instagram posts and laughing at the dumb shit I ran across. Then I saw her, or rather, a picture of her. The caption on it read: *On my way to hang with my Uncle Leland tonight*, followed by three of those heart eyes emojis. I must've stared at that picture for three or four minutes before I hopped up from the bed and into the shower. I moved as fast as I could, but it still took me a minute to get out the door.

SHE OPENED THE DOOR, her eyes wide with surprise, a smile on her lips. My mom was a god-tier beauty. There seriously wasn't a woman past or present that came close to her. Well, there was one.

Just one.

"I got your text saying you were on your way, and I know I buzzed you in the gate, but I still can't believe you're really here! I wanna hug you. Would that be okay?" she rambled.

I nodded, but I couldn't make myself smile.

She reached up, pulling me into her arms, and I involuntarily wrapped mine around her. My mom had this smell, not perfume, but just...*her*, and it reminded me of when I was a kid and she'd hug me. The shit almost made me tear up, but before it did, I backed out of the hug and shoved my hands into the pockets of my jeans.

"Uh...I ain't too late, am I?" I asked. "For dinner, I mean."

"Oh, no! We've been catching up with Ella. We just sat

down to eat. Have you met Ella, Leland's niece? I can't remember if you two have been in the same room at the same time."

I shook my head. I'd turned down every family gathering invitation my mom had extended to me over the years since she became a McClain, so I didn't know much of anybody in that family. I mean, I knew *of* them, of course, especially Big South. I just didn't *know them*, know them.

She grabbed my hand. "Well, come meet her and her friend."

I let her guide me through the foyer into the huge dining room —big, round white table, white chairs, a chandelier. The room screamed money. Leland McClain had been in the league a lot longer than me and this house showed it.

"My Armand made it!" my mom gushed.

Leland gave me a nod as he bounced one of his sons on his knee. The kid was cute, *all* the kids—Little Leland, Layla, and the twins, Saint and Houston—were cute even if they did look like their dad, and I did manage to give them a smile as my mom told them to greet me.

"...and this is Ella and her friend Carlos," my mom said. "Ella, Carlos, this is my oldest son, Armand."

"I'm familiar with him," Ella said. Her voice was heavier than most women, real throaty. "Hi, Armand."

"'Sup?" I replied, my eyes glued to her. I couldn't even make myself stop looking at her when I returned her friend's greeting. Shit, I didn't bother to glance at him until we were halfway through the meal, which my ass inhaled.

When I say my mom could burn, I mean she could *burn*. I hadn't tasted anything as good as the fried pork chops, collard greens, and pinto beans she served me in a long ass time.

"Dang, you was hungry, huh?" a little voice said.

I looked up to see that it was Little Leland roasting me, his eyes wide, his ridiculous head of hair all over the place. He was sitting directly across from me in between his dad and Ella. I smiled at him and said, "I was, plus our mom can cook, man."

"I know that," he retorted, rolling his eyes and making Ella laugh.

"That's because you're the smartest eight-year-old on the planet!" Ella crooned, kissing the top of his head. The little dude grinned before leaning into her and wrapping his arms around her. Seemed like little dude had a crush on his older cousin. Shit, so did I.

"Little Leland's been asking about you ever since I told him you lived here now. I'm glad you finally came to see us, El," Leland said.

From over the rim of my glass of water, I watched Ella's facial expression change, her smile sliding into a somber mask. "I was... I've been trying to get settled, but I'll be visiting more. I promise," she said.

"Good, then maybe your dad will calm his ass down. He's been calling me every day for a report and I ain't had nothing to tell him," Leland informed her. "He be trying not to call and bother you."

Ella nodded. "Yeah, he worries too much. I'm good."

"I can see that," Leland affirmed, "but don't be a stranger. We're here for you. The whole point of moving here was so that you could make a fresh start while still being close to family. We got you."

She gave him a small smile and a nod. "I'll do better, Uncle Leland. Besides, I miss my little cousins. Gotta come spend time with them. They're growing up too fast!"

Leland shook his head. "Who you telling?"

The conversations went on between everyone but me. I was an observer at heart. I liked watching and analyzing people, and my mom understood that about me. I could tell she was just happy I was there. When you're an observer, you notice a lot of things about people even if they think they're hiding them. Like, as much as I had to fight to stomach being in the same hemisphere as Leland McClain, I knew he really loved my mom. By watching my mom, I could see she was truly happy for the first time in a long time. I could see that the kids were well cared for. And Ella? Although anyone could easily see how much she was loved and adored, I could see what was behind her smile. I could virtually feel her sadness.

SIX

ELLA

"So, are you going to tell me what that was about?" Carlos asked as he drove us back to my place.

"What? What do you mean?" I replied, my eyes on the darkened scenery outside the windshield.

"Ella J, you know what I'm talking about! Stop tryna play dumb!"

I shifted my eyes to him as he kept his on the road. "I'm not playing dumb."

He shook his head. "You are the smartest woman I know, always have been. You know what the hell I'm referring to."

I stared at him blankly.

"Armand Daniels!"

I lifted an eyebrow. "What about him?"

"You *know* what! Are you really going to sit there and pretend you didn't notice him staring at you damn near the entire evening?"

"You're exaggerating. He didn't stare at me the entire evening."

"Ella, if you don't stop playing!"

I finally broke character, allowing myself to laugh, which in turn made him laugh as he mumbled, "I really hate your ass."

I rolled my eyes. "Uh-huh, I know you do. Anyway, I did notice him looking at me."

"And?"

"And I looked at him. Didn't you?"

"What? Because I'm gay I gotta just stare at any nigga I run across?"

"No, just the fine ones, and I know you aren't gonna lie and say Armand Daniels isn't fine."

"I'm not one to lie, and I ain't starting now. Him being fine is common knowledge. I knew that before tonight. I will admit that seeing him up close was...nice."

"It sure was. Those eyes? Those dimples? That body? If he wasn't so damn crazy, I think I could like him."

"Yeah, the nigga is nuts. You can see it in his eyes," Carlos agreed.

"Is that what you saw in his eyes? Craziness?"

"Hell yeah. Didn't you?"

"No. To me, he just seemed lost, out of place. Crazy, too, but more than anything, I saw sorrow in his eyes. I have enough of that to deal with myself. So as fine as he is, I can't go there with him. Besides, he's family by marriage."

"That ain't really family, Ella, but I get it. That temper of his would have me flying back here to kick his ass if he got down wrong with you."

I scoffed. "You'd have to get in line behind my dad and all of my uncles. Me and him would be a FEMA level disaster. Even if I could look past his major anger issues, the family dynamics would be too much. It's a no go on me and Armand Daniels."

"I know that's right!"

ARMAND

For some stupid ass reason, I waited until I was on the team plane on my way to Oklahoma to check the email Mr. Charles sent me. So I was looking confused as hell when I saw its contents, just three words: *Intermittent Explosive Disorder*.

Huh?

Why would this nigga send me an email with only three words in it?

Lifting my head, I glanced around the plane to see most of my teammates laughing and talking to each other. I was sitting next to Sean Drummond, a rookie who didn't talk much, which was good with me because I didn't want to be talked to. He wasn't nosy, either. As I sat there, eyebrows wrinkled up while I stared at the message, Drummond kept his eyes on his own phone and AirPods in his ears, which gave me an idea. Since I was tired as hell from gearing up to do something I hated—flying—I did a quick YouTube search using the plane's WiFi, pulled my headphones over my ears, got comfortable in my seat, and hit play. Some dude who called himself a doctor started explaining what Intermittent Explosive Disorder was—sudden episodes of aggressive or violent behavior. He said these outbursts were often disproportionate to the intensity of the situation. I opened my eyes and paused the video, glancing around to make sure no one was paying attention to me. Like, I didn't want anyone to know I was listening to this stuff, listening to this dude talk about...me. Mr. Charles sent this to me because these three words described me. When shit made me mad, it made me *too* mad, so mad that I broke things or hurt people without even realizing it. I wasn't sure how knowing this, having a name to put on what I was, was supposed to make me feel. Was I supposed to be relieved? Was I supposed to accept this shit? Was I supposed to be upset? Well, I *was* upset. I was pissed at the therapist for sending this stupid email and at myself for reading it hours before a game. I wanted to tear some shit up, to punch something or somebody, to—

Fuck!

What was wrong with me? Why was I so mad?

As soon as those questions popped into my head, I let my eyes fall back to my phone and the paused video.

Intermittent Explosive Disorder—that was what was wrong with me.

Shit.

YOU GOT THERAPY TOMORROW. *Don't miss it.*

That text from Nathan Moore came just as I stepped in my Oklahoma City hotel room. We lost, and losing always pissed me off. So seeing that message was especially irritating to me. I needed to get out and find me a drink and some pussy. Pussy usually calmed my nerves at least a little bit, but in addition to being pissed off, I was also tired as shit.

Exhausted.

Then there was the fact that partaking of random pussy had gotten me in trouble in the past. See, this one lying-ass chick accused me of taking it from her, and while I was able to prove she was lying, I was super careful about that shit now.

So instead, I dropped my phone and body onto the bed and closed my eyes. The only thought in my head?

I wasn't going to no more fucking therapy.

I WENT TO THERAPY.

I didn't *want* to go but I did want to talk to Alvin Charles about his email. I needed to know what I was supposed to do with this new information. So yeah, I went back to that office, sat in one of those beige chairs in the waiting area, my knee bouncing, my thoughts loud in the excruciating silence as I waited for my name to be called.

Again, I was the only person in the waiting area except for the receptionist, but she didn't really count since she was behind the glass in her little booth. I hated being alone as much as I liked it. I hated silence as much as I needed it. I was just...confusing, even to myself. Not much about me made sense other than the talent for the game I loved that I was born with, and I was pretty publicly going to fuck that up if I didn't—

"Mr. Daniels."

My head snatched around to face the owner of the voice, my eyes colliding with the much shorter, bearded black man standing in the doorway of the inner office. Biting my bottom lip, I stood and was sitting across from him in less than a minute.

I'd barely settled on the loveseat when he said, "Good to see you again, Mr. Daniels."

"Armand. You can call me Armand," I replied.

"Okay, Armand...I trust that you received my email?"

I dropped my eyes from his face. "Yeah, I got it. That's why I'm here."

He nodded. "What did you think?"

I shrugged, resting an elbow on the arm of my seat. "What am I supposed to think?"

"You're supposed to think whatever you think. Let's try this: what was the first thing that popped into your mind when you read the words in that email?"

My eyes roamed the room before landing on his face again. "Confusion. I was confused, and then..."

"And then?"

I sighed. "And then I listened to this dude on YouTube explain what it means, and I… it pissed me off, made me want to fuck everything and everyone around me up."

"Did you?" he asked, his voice ridiculously calm.

I frowned. "Did I what?"

"Did you fuck anything up?"

"No…I just went to sleep. Woke up, got off the plane, lost the game…"

"And you stopped being angry after you went to sleep?"

"No, I was still mad, just stopped wanting to fuck things up."

"Hmm, why do you think that YouTube video made you mad?"

I shrugged again. "Man, I don't know. I didn't want to hear that shit and think it applied to me. I ain't wanna believe I had something wrong with me with a long-ass name attached to it." This whole thing, talking to him, was mad uncomfortable, made me feel like my skin didn't fit right again. I was about to just get up and leave when he posed another question.

"What makes you think it applied to you—Intermittent Explosive Disorder, I mean?"

Sitting up straight, I felt my heart rate increase with the volume of my voice. "Because you sent that email! Ain't that why you sent it?! Because I got that shit?!"

"I sent it because based on what I know about you, you fit the description of that particular disorder. What I'm asking is why do *you* think it applies to you?"

"Because it does! Because I do the shit that goes along with it. I get mad, *real* mad about little shit and big shit and all shit! I'm mad right now! I wanna fuck you and this office up because being here and talking about this stuff makes my damn skin crawl. I feel like I'm choking and drowning at the same time just from being here. I hate this!"

The room fell silent as Mr. Charles stared at me, calm, quiet, seemingly unbothered by me screaming and yelling at him. Hell, I was literally vibrating and there he sat, unmoved, completely composed.

I let out a harsh breath before collapsing against the back of my seat. "Why am I like this, man? Why am I like this?" I muttered.

"Together, we're going to find out, and together, we're going to figure out the best way for you to manage this. I just need you to commit, *really commit*, to doing the work," he replied.

After a moment or two of me staring down at the floor, I nodded. "I'll try."

SEVEN

ELLA

"Hi, Ella. This is Tippy. Of course you know the anniversary of my Jackson's passing is coming up, and I'm sure you want to give some input on this year's celebration of his life, as always. Give me a call back so we can discuss it. I know you're in St. Louis, but you're welcome to stay with me in Minneapolis while you're here for the celebration. Hope to talk to you soon."

The voicemail ended, and minutes later, I found myself still sitting at my dining room table, my breakfast untouched, the screen of my phone black, and tears streaming down my face. I just wanted to move on, to no longer be tied to Jackson or the memories that were tethered to him. I wanted to be more than just *his* girl, the one he left behind. I wanted my damn life back, my pre-Jackson "On One" Reynolds life back. But everything I did or was before and after him had been conflated with that singular relationship, as if I wasn't a college graduate, a professional model, a damn individual. Hell, as if I wasn't the daughter and niece of celebrities, as if my name on its own carried no weight.

Two years.

Only two years of my life were spent as this man's girlfriend. Were they an intense two years? Yes. Did it make sense that his considerable fans had become obsessed with our pairing? I guess. But he was gone, I was still here, and I had moved on. Mentally, emotionally, even geographically, I had moved on. So why hadn't everyone else?

My phone awakened so abruptly that I actually jumped in my chair, my eyes narrowing as the screen resurrected and my mother's name appeared on it. An involuntary groan escaped my mouth. What next? Was some high school bully going to message me on social media offering me the chance to "be my own boss"? Damn!

I knew myself well enough to know that if I didn't get in front of this feeling of irritation that was slowly overtaking me, I'd soon find myself in a dark place, in a hole that was hell to dig out of, so I picked up my phone, ignoring the new voicemail alert, and sent Mother Erica a simple text: *Help.*

ARMAND

This felt weird, probably seemed odd to my mom, too, but it was what I wanted even if I wasn't sure why. I'd been seeing Mr. Charles once a week for a whole month. He suggested we bump it up to twice weekly, but I told him I just couldn't do that shit. I swear I'd end up scratching my own eyeballs out if I had to talk about this stuff anymore than I already was.

We'd quickly gotten to the bottom of my issues, not that it would take a rocket scientist to figure it out. My anger was a side effect of having watched nigga after nigga beat on my mom. I guess seeing that kind of stuff would mess anyone up. Alvin Charles said trauma affects people in different ways. Some find themselves in the midst of an addiction, others grapple with depression or anxiety. But many, like me, see their trauma manifested through anger and violence. Those who might not have been fortunate enough to have the protections afforded me because of my profession find themselves in and out of jail. So I knew the *why*. Moving forward, we would work on the *how*—how to deal with the trauma, how to face my issues, how to be better.

Crazy enough, I actually wanted to be better but was still uncomfortable with the whole process, with talking about my shit. But back to the beautiful woman standing in front of me with a bewildered look on her face, her eyes sliding from the shiny foyer floor beneath my feet to meet mine. The front door was still open behind me, and as she stood there mute, I figured I'd stunned her into silence.

"Can I close the door...or you want me to leave?" I slowly asked.

"What?" she squeaked with furrowed brows. "Oh, no! I mean, you can close it. I'm just...are you sure?"

"Uh, if the offer still stands. You said the cottage was mine to use when I'm in St. Louis. I been staying at the Sable because I'm kinda leery about getting a place just to get traded and have to move. I was thinking I could just stay here."

I could see the tears in my mom's eyes as she reached up and cupped my face in her hands. "From the second I found out you were traded to the Cyclones, I was hoping you'd stay here with us. I just can't believe it, though."

I stared down at her and managed to give her an almost smile. "Believe it."

"Boogie—"

She was cut off by a loud scream from one of her kids. Her head snatched away from me and back. "Pull your car around back. I'll meet you at the cottage in a few minutes. Let me go see who is trying to kill who this time."

I nodded and watched her leave the foyer, moving deeper into the house. Then I headed out the front door to my SUV and drove around to the back of the mansion where the garages were located. Situated at the rear of the property, far beyond the pool and gym complex, stood a much-smaller replica of the main house. When she finally let me inside with all four kids in tow, I saw that it contained a small living room, one bedroom, an eat-in kitchen, and a bathroom, about six-hundred square feet of space decorated in white and gray and dark blue. It was nice, uncluttered, neutral. I liked it. I liked it a lot.

As I moved from room to room, I could hear tiny footsteps behind me—Little Leland. That actually made me smile. When I returned to the living room, my mom was still standing in the front doorway wearing a track suit, a look of worry on her face. Little Layla stood next to her, holding onto one of her legs. The twins sat in a stroller. They could both walk but they were still small, and I was sure they couldn't keep up with the other two.

"So...will this work for you?" my mom asked, her voice an octave or two higher than usual.

"He likes it. I can tell," Little Leland piped up.

I glanced down at him and gave him a grin. "How you know, man?"

Little Leland shrugged his shoulders as he looked up at me. "I just do."

Chuckling, I replied, "You're right. I do." Returning my attention to my mom, I added, "This is nice. I can vibe with it. Thanks for letting me stay here."

"You're my son. Of course I'm going to let you stay here, Boogie."

I nodded, but I felt uncomfortable. Something about hearing her say I was her son with these other kids present felt...strange, and I didn't even know why.

"Well, we'll let you get settled. I know you're grown and probably want to live totally separate from us, but you are always welcome to eat with us or just hang out anytime, okay?"

I nodded again and said, "Okay," but I had no intention of hanging out in that house.

ELLA

I avoided everyone, including my wonderful family, because of Jackson's death, or rather, my connection to him. It was the fear of having them bring up the relationship, or more truthfully, the image we portrayed. I just didn't want to hear or think about any of it. I was over it and him, and I felt like shit for feeling that way, so the last thing I wanted or needed was to be reminded of any of it. However, there I was, sitting in my car outside my uncle's home, preparing to visit his family.

Closing my eyes, I sighed before reading Mother Erica's response to my "help" text.

I know you have a tough few weeks ahead of you, but remember who you are. Not only do you have generations of ancestors of the greatest ilk standing with you, but you also have a family that loves you. Seek comfort with your kin, daughter.

I trusted this woman who'd helped me back away from total self-destruction and took every syllable of each of her words to heart. So, I slid my phone into my purse and left my vehicle. An hour or so later, I was still there, sitting on my uncle's overstuffed living room sofa smiling so widely at my cousins as they climbed all over him that my cheeks hurt. My stomach was happy because of the three slices of pound cake I'd eaten, a masterpiece mailed to my uncle from our Aunt Ever. And the heaviness that weighed me down earlier was gone.

"Kim! You still in the bathroom?!" Uncle Leland shouted as either Saint or Houston took a seat on his forehead. Those boys were going on two, and I still couldn't tell them apart.

"No!" Aunt Kim called back. "I ran over to Armand's to take him some cake. Just getting back." She appeared in the living room, smiling.

"Oh, I forgot you said you were gonna do that," Uncle Leland said.

"He stays that close to you guys?" I asked.

"My big brother lives back there!" Little Leland announced. He was wearing his father's huge shoes, struggling to walk in them. I followed his little finger to the wall of patio doors that allowed a breathtaking view of the patio, pool, yard, and guest cottage.

"Oh, he does?" I asked, my eyebrows peaked.

Aunt Kim smiled proudly. "Yes! He just moved in the other day!"

My eyes remained glued to the cottage as I said, "That's cool."

"It truly is. I mean, he hasn't really been interacting with us, but I'm just happy he's near me. Armand isn't the easiest person to get along with, but I love him and I've missed him."

I nodded, turning my attention back to my cousins.

EIGHT

ELLA

"Hey, Daddy," was how I answered my dad's early morning FaceTime call. I was still in bed, burrowed beneath the covers, a silk bonnet on my head and sleep fogging my brain, but I knew to shake myself awake and take this call.

"Hey, Princess. How you feeling this morning?" he responded.

I smiled as I took in his image on my phone's screen. He'd called and texted me several times since the move here, but this was the first time I'd seen his face in well over a month. He looked the same—handsome and big and strong.

Always, *always* my hero.

"I'm good." A tear escaped my eye and I almost groaned.

"What's wrong, Ella?" he asked, his voice soft and gentle, which made me full-on cry.

"Baby girl, talk to me. Tell me what's wrong," he pleaded.

It took me a moment, but I finally pulled myself together, moving to sit with my back against the tufted headboard as I wiped my face with my free hand. I wanted to lie, but I just didn't have the energy to. So I blurted, "I'm just stressed. Mom keeps trying to contact me, I'm flying to Paris for Fashion Week next week, and after that is the anniversary of One's death and I just don't want to even think about that. I want to move on with my life, Daddy!"

I started crying again, and my dad was gracious enough to let the well dry up before he spoke.

"Hey, listen...*move on*. I know that seems hard because things are so public, but you can do it. You're already doing it."

"But...there's going to be another memorial service this year. I'm expected to be there, and I just don't want to go. I don't want to be a part of that anymore."

"Then don't. Princess, you're worried about what outside people will think of you if you don't go but you shouldn't be. You grew up in the spotlight, so you know they're going to think whatever the hell they want to no matter what you do. So do what's best for you unapologetically. Hey, Jo wants to talk to you."

I sniffled. "Okay."

Jo's pretty face came into view. "Hey, Ella. Just wanted to chime in. If there's one thing I've learned, it's that the only opinions that matter when it comes to you and your decisions belong to the people they directly impact. In your case, that's you and only you. You've mourned. You've worked on your healing. Now it's time for you to live."

"Thank you, Jo." I replied, my voice still shaky. "Thank you, too, Daddy. I love y'all."

"We love you more, and as for your mom, you need me to handle her? Because I will." That was my daddy.

"No, if you contact her, it'll only trigger her craziness. I can handle it," I said.

"All right. Now go live, Princess," he said.

"I will, Daddy. I will."

. . .

CARLOS: *I know that ain't you I see sitting court side at the Cyclones game. When you start watching basketball?*

Grinning, I replied to his text: *Since my uncle gave me a ticket. Why? Something wrong with me watching basketball?*

Carlos: *It's something wrong with you watching it without me. I'm jealous! And you're sitting next to your aunt! You know how I feel about her skin!*

Me: *I know, I know. It really is flawless.*

Him: *Facts!*

I was about to reply to him when the players started returning to the court. Halftime was over, and I was ready for the action to resume. So was Kim, who was a pro at attending the games. I actually flinched when she started yelling, but then I smiled.

"Let's go, Cyclones! You got this, McClain, Daniels! Let's whoop some ass!" Kim screamed. Little Leland and Layla, who were sitting behind us with Kim's cousin Zabrina, were yelling, too. The twins were home with Kim's mom.

Uncle Leland was the first to hear his family. I watched as he smiled and waved at them. Then my eyes found Armand—tall, toasty brown, hazel-eyed Armand. He smiled at his mother, although his smile was subdued compared to my uncle's; then his eyes fell on me, and I swear a shiver raced up my spine. From that moment forward, *he* was my focus. I watched his every move, could probably count the beads of sweat on his face at one point. Yes, he was handsome, no big surprise considering his mother's beauty, but beyond that, he was just...enigmatic and magnetic. He was troubled, everyone with eyes could see that, and those with a gift for empathy could literally feel it. He was troubled *and* he was trouble, but there was something about him, an undercurrent of mystery that I had an overwhelmingly visceral desire to solve. Did I want to fuck him? Uh, duh! But I also wanted to learn him, to understand him, maybe even like him.

Maybe.

I was so deep in thought about this one player, that when a player from the opposing team came barreling toward me, I yelped. I didn't see him coming at all, and he barely missed crashing into me. My hand flew to my chest as if to calm my thumping heart as I nodded, assuring Kim and everyone else around me that I was okay. When I finally returned my attention to the court, my eyes collided with his—Armand's. Imagine my shock and horror when, in the middle of the game, he bulldozed his way down the court with the ball, passed it, and then rammed his body into the guy who'd almost trampled me.

ARMAND

I dragged my ass into the house and fell on the sofa after another therapy session, tired as shit from not having an explanation for trying to clothesline Patrick O'Reilly, a player on the Heat, one of my old teams. The media, my coach, and Mr. Charles assumed it was because dude came close to falling on my mom. I mean, that was half of it, I guess. So I went with that, but the truth? That big, burly motherfucker came closer to hurting Ella McClain than my mom. I couldn't admit that, though because everybody knew she was On One's girl. Yeah, dude was gone, had offed himself right in front of her, but everybody knew she was off-limits. Did I want her? Hell fucking yes. I had it bad for Ella McClain, just like any dude with a working dick would, only I wasn't going to go there with her.

But I wanted to.

So damn bad.

Anyway, everyone thinking it was about my mom, including my mom, made it more acceptable. Yeah, I got ejected from the game and was hit with a Fifty-K fine, but there was no talk of trading me. Mr. Charles worked with me on ways to contain my anger, even if it was warranted, but that was only after he explained that accidents happen, and that dude didn't *try* to run into anybody. Then he suggested me taking some medicine, to which I said *fuck no*. I wasn't taking nothing that might slow down or fuck up my game. Shit, I was getting mad just thinking about that.

Moving to lie down on the too-short sofa, I decided to check out IG, the first picture on my screen one of Ella McClain outside a private plane, shades covering her eyes and her hair wind-blown. The caption read: *On my way to Paris Fashion Week!*

Damn, she was fine. Like, the finest.

I was still on IG when a soft knock sounded at my door. It was probably my mom bringing me some food, and since I wasn't stupid enough to turn her food down, I hopped to my feet to answer it. On the other side stood Little Leland and Layla, both gazing up at me with wide eyes.

Before I could speak, Layla asked, "Can we come in?" Little Leland quickly parroted her.

"Uh, yeah," I muttered. What the hell?

They both basically skipped into the cottage and sat together in the white chair that matched the white sofa. I dropped to the sofa, asking, "Y'all okay? I mean, where's your mom? She know you here?"

"No. She told us we shouldn't bother you, but you're our brother just like Saint and Houston, right?" Layla, the obvious spokesperson, quizzed me.

"Oh," I replied, "uh...yes?"

"You wanna come play games with us? We got a PS5 and 2K. We'll let you win," Little Leland offered.

Now *that* made me laugh. "Really, little guy? You know I play ball, right?"

He nodded. "So does my daddy, and I beat him all the time."

"Oh, word? You that good?"

"We both are!" Layla trilled.

I chuckled. They were cute as hell, no lie.

Another knock came at the door followed by, "Armand, you in there?"

My mom.

"Yes, ma'am. Come in!" I shouted in return.

She opened the door, her eyes searching until they fell on Leland and Layla. "You guys are not supposed to be here! Sorry, Boogie. They know better. Y'all come on!"

"It's all good," I said, watching as they both scrambled from the chair and ran out the door. "They're...cute and apparently, they plan on letting me win at 2K."

She shook her head. "They're obsessed with video games. It's a problem. Hey, you okay? After what happened at the game, I mean?"

"Yeah, I'm fine. I'm...gonna take some deep breaths or something next time, throat my chakras. You know, tai my chi." I ended the statement with a shrug.

My mom smiled. "I'm glad you're okay."

I nodded, watched her leave, and resumed my IG browsing.

NINE

ELLA

My mother was in Paris, too.

Not only was she in Paris, but she was also staying down the hall from me in Claude DuMont's grand home. I wasn't sure who I was angrier at, Claude for insisting I stay with him during Fashion Week knowing he'd also invited my mother, or my mother for failing to disclose this information in one of her many texts or voicemails. Either way, I was so pissed I closed myself up in the *Naomi Campbell* room, as Claude called it, for most of my time there, only emerging for meals, and that morning, to walk in Claude's and Thierry Mugler's shows. Afterwards, as I scrubbed makeup off my face, a text popped up on my phone from my mother stating: *You did well, but it looks like you've gained weight.*

So yeah, I wasn't trying to interact with her at all.

The *Naomi* bedroom was huge and just as elaborately furnished and adorned as the rest of the house that resembled a museum. Well, it *was* a museum in a way, as it housed tons of antiques, and an entire room was dedicated to showcasing some of the iconic pieces Claude had created during his forty-year career. I usually loved staying here, one of the perks of being me, DuMont's current favorite model, a title he'd once given to my mother. I suppose my knowledge of their decades-long friendship should've clued me in on this little ambush, but it didn't, and that was largely because Jackson's memorial was the very next week. In lieu of calling his mother, I'd texted her to let her know whatever she planned for the celebration of his life would be fine with me. I neglected to tell her I had no plans of attending, but I didn't.

I couldn't.

A knock at the bedroom door startled me, but I didn't move to answer. Another knock followed it, and then I heard her voice. "Ella, darling... are you in there?" It was my mother, of course.

Still no response from me.

There were no more knocks until about twenty minutes later, these accompanied by a man's thick French accent. "Mon ange! Are you in there, chérie?"

"I am if you're alone," I answered.

"I am alone, mon amour. Can I enter?"

Standing from where I'd been seated on the side of the bed, I held my silk robe closed and crossed the room, unlocking the door and allowing the older man entrance. Claude DuMont was a handsome, sexually fluid man with copper skin, a bald head, and a salt and pepper beard who stood an inch or so taller than me. He wore jeans and what could only be described as a red and orange blouse, red paint on his fingernails, and high-top converse sneakers on his feet. He was...different, unique, a complete artist. Born in the French West Indies and raised in southern France, Claude was one of the most successful fashion designers in the world, an especially noteworthy feat for a black man. He was also kind and giving and philanthropic, an icon in the diaspora. I adored him, but he'd crossed the line.

"Je suis désolé," he crooned as he took a seat in one of the ornate chairs situated in the sitting area of the room.

"You are not forgiven and I'm leaving," I said.

"Chérie, don't go. I thought you were staying for another week!" His disappointment was more than evident, but it couldn't surpass mine.

"I was, but I don't want to be around her, and you know that."

"Mon—"

"I'm leaving, Claude, and I honestly don't know when I'll be ready to even talk to you again."

"Ella," he groaned, "please understand my motives. You see, my dear mother was everything to me. She taught me to sew. Maman believed in me before I believed in myself, but she died before I saw real success. I miss her every day, chérie. I merely want you to appreciate your mother while she is still here on Earth with you. I do not want you to live with regrets. I mean no harm."

I followed his eyes to the portrait hanging above the fireplace in the bedroom, a beautiful rendering of Laurette DuMont, his mother. "She was breathtaking, Claude, but unlike my mother, her beauty extended to her heart. I understand your sentiment, but it simply does not apply to me. When people say you should cherish your mother, they don't mean mothers like mine. I can't stay, and I'll need time to decide where our friendship will go from here."

He stared up at me, his deep brown eyes full of sadness as he nodded his acceptance.

ARMAND

I'd been following Ella McClain on IG for a couple of years. I never liked any of her posts or made any comments, but there wasn't a picture I hadn't seen...and admired. When On One was still alive and they were together, I used to think about how lucky he was. Ella was a class act—beautiful, successful, and she wasn't always shaking her ass on the Gram. I could tell she was loyal, too. When I saw that I had a DM from her, I damn near shit myself. It was only one word, but still, she sent me a message! Me! Maybe I wasn't imagining her staring at me during our last home game.

Maybe.

Her message read: *Hi.*

I replied with: *Hi.*

Her: *I just followed you back.*

I frowned, rushed to check my notifications, and wondered how I'd overlooked that. She'd followed me like five minutes earlier.

Me: *Appreciate that.*

Her: *It was my pleasure.*

Shit!

I was trying to calm my excited ass down and think of how to respond when she sent: *I'll be at dinner at my uncle's tonight. Will I see you there?*

I hadn't planned on it, but those plans immediately changed.

Me: *Yeah, I'll be there.*

I glanced at the time. Shit, it was already time for dinner.

Me: *Where are you?*

Her: *In my uncle's driveway. See you soon.*

I didn't reply to that last message. Instead, I jumped my ass up from the couch and got myself together. Ten minutes later, I was heading across the backyard to my mom's house.

I WAS STANDING at one of the patio doors at the back of the house looking like a damn stalker as I knocked, but if Ella McClain was going to be in there, so was I.

"Boogie?" my mom said, voice shrill as she slid the door open. "Is...are you okay?"

"Uh, yeah...I just thought I'd come...uh...visit y'all for a minute," I answered her sounding as dumb as I felt.

Her eyes lit up and I actually felt kind of bad because I knew she thought I was trying to repair our relationship, and although I kind of wanted that, my main objective was to breathe the same air as my mother's husband's niece. Was that fucked up? Probably so, but it was what it was. I liked Ella, like really, *really* liked her.

"Well, come in! Little Leland and Layla will be excited to see you! Oh! We're about to eat dinner. Wanna join us?"

"Uh, yeah...yeah, I could eat."

Grasping my hand, she said, "Great!"

She was so happy that it made me smile. Some things just don't change, and I'd always loved seeing my mom happy. It was a rare sight when I was growing up.

"Oh, and Ella's having dinner with us, too!" my mom gushed as she pulled me to the dining room.

"Word? That's cool," I replied, and then there she was, already seated at the table looking like a damn dream come true. She was talking to my mom's husband as we entered the room. When they both looked up, I gave Leland a nod and locked eyes with Ella as I said, "Hi."

In return, she did this little wave and resumed talking to her uncle.

WHAT THE FUCK was with this chick? She sent me that message letting me know she'd be at dinner and spent the whole evening acting like I wasn't there. She was talkative as hell about her trip to Paris, walking the runway, and all that stuff, which I can admit was interesting, but she didn't even look my way after giving me that tiny wave. Little Leland, on the other hand, couldn't get enough of my ass. Layla either. They sat on either side of me telling me all kinds of random shit. At one point, my mom tried to get them to leave me alone, but I told her they were good. They were growing on me. That was probably why I agreed to play 2K with them after dinner.

Ella had already left when I sat down on the floor in what the kids called the game room and grabbed a controller. Little Leland was my first opponent with Layla serving as spectator. Leland Sr. sat on the sofa holding the twins, but he didn't say anything to me, and I appreciated that. I played with them for about an hour before I left. Little Leland and Layla, who took turns battling me, each choosing to play as their dad while I chose Drayveon Walker, were actually good. Of course I *let* them win, but they were almost real competition. I'd barely made it through my door when an IG notification popped up on my phone. Ella had DM'd me again:

My number is 555-555-1269. Call me tomorrow morning.

Call her? After she'd ignored my ass all night, she wanted me to call her? What the fuck?

Me: *Okay.*

I mean, yeah, I was going to call her.

Hell-yeah I was.

TEN

ELLA

Today was both the anniversary of Jackson's death and the day of the annual memorial. There was also another Cyclones home game tonight. I was going to the game, and I was determined to enjoy every second of it. I was taking my dad's advice and living for *me*. I was so serious about it that I'd texted Jackson's mom in the middle of the night to let her know I couldn't make it.

Her reply: *Why?*

I didn't provide an answer.

I *couldn't*.

I awoke early that morning to take a call from my agent regarding a booking for a magazine spread. Afterwards, I fixed breakfast and contacted Rhode, my St. Louis makeup artist, to see if she could fit me in before the game. I didn't go to any event without my hair laid and face beat. I'd had my hair braided before Fashion Week and it still looked good. All I'd have to do was make sure my edges were on point.

I'd just hung up with Rhode when a call from an unknown number came through. "Hello?" I answered as I stuffed a piece of avocado toast in my mouth.

"Hey, good morning."

That voice! That damn voice! Armand Daniels' voice was deep and somehow smooth and rough at the same time. He had my coochie throbbing at dinner last night just from saying hi to me.

"Good morning, Mr. Daniels. You're up early."

"Gotta game tonight. Leaving for the shoot around in like thirty minutes."

"Ah, I see. Well, thank you for taking the time to call me."

"No problem. Uh...why did you want me to call you?"

"Because I think you like me. Do you?"

"Do I what?"

"Do you like me, Mr. Daniels?"

"Why? You like me or something?"

I smiled, took a sip of orange juice, and admitted, "I do."

"Word? Well, yeah...I like you."

"That's good to know. Mr.—"

"Armand. You can call me Armand."

"I can't call you Boogie?" I teased.

"Full disclosure, you can call me whatever you want to call me, and I won't be mad."

"Ohhh, so you *like* me like me? That's good to know, too."

"Is it?"

"It is. I know you've got to go."

"Yeah...I can call you later if you want."

"I want."

"Bet. Oh, and Ella?"

"Yes?"

"You coming to the game tonight?"

"Yes, I plan to be there."

"Don't sit on the floor. I don't wanna have to kick anyone else's ass for running into you."

"Uh, I don't think the guy *tried* to run into me."

"Maybe he didn't, but accident or not, I'll fuck the next dude up, too. Don't sit on the floor tonight."

"Uh...okay," I said slowly.

ARMAND

I loved game days, especially home game days. Sure, I still got a little nervous before a game, but there was nothing like going to war for a win. I hated losing, but I loved the battle. I was good at this shit, too, a versatile player, which was why I was still in the league. Yeah, I was seen as a liability, but I was also seen as an asset.

I usually played power forward but possessed small forward skills as well. I was mean at making shots in the paint, but I wasn't shit to sneeze at beyond the three-point line either. I wasn't just being cocky. It was the truth. I knew it and so did everybody else.

This game, though? This game was a cluster fuck if I'd ever seen one. We were playing like shit. I mean, the Bulls were putting their collective feet up our collective asses. At home! The shit was embarrassing as hell, and I could feel my anger building with each second that ticked off the clock and we were still down.

Then my teammate, Riley, lost control of the ball while heading downcourt. It was quickly recovered by Tim Olguin from the Bulls who made a three-pointer. That did it. Somebody's ass needed to be kicked ASAP, and my hands were itching to pummel Riley. We were going to lose. Wasn't but a damn minute left in the game and we seemed to be playing worse and worse.

Fuck!

Coach called a timeout, and while I stood there with ice in my veins, my right eye twitching, and malice in my soul, I looked up, my gaze crashing into hers, *Ella's*. As I stared at her, she slowly shook her head and I felt...I don't know, chastised? Like if I kicked Riley's ass, I'd disappoint her, and for some reason, the thought of disappointing her felt wrong, strongly unappealing.

"Daniels, you're out for now. You look exhausted," I heard Coach say. "You've been playing your ass off tonight."

I frowned, wanting to protest. I didn't feel tired at all, but again, I looked up and into Ella's eyes. Another headshake from her. So I just nodded at Coach and rode the bench for the remainder of the game.

THIS TEAM REALLY WAS DIFFERENT. In the past, it seemed like my teammates fed my anger, but these dudes? Although we lost, they each made it a point to tell me it was a good game for *me*, that *my* performance was on point. I honestly didn't know what to do with that, so I just nodded.

As I left the locker room, headed to the cryo room, I texted Ella: *Why you shake your head at me?*

I'd made it to the room and had eased into the ice bath by the time she replied: *Because you looked like you were about to kill someone.*

Me: *Nah. I was just gonna fuck someone up.*

Her: *That would've been counterintuitive, Armand.*

Me: *Being intuitive ain't exactly my claim to fame.*

Her: *I know but that can change.*

Me: *So you tryna change a nigga?*

Her: *No. Never that.*

Me: *Seems like it to me.*

Her: *What I'm trying to do is help you see the bigger picture. You could've kicked someone's ass and you still would've lost. The only difference would be you'd have lost and owed a fine, possible suspension, lost your job. See what I mean?*

I rolled my eyes.

Me: *Yeah, I see. You sound like my agent.*

Her: *I also sound right, don't I?*

I grinned. I liked her energy, that bad bitch energy.

Me: *Yeah. You do.*

ELEVEN

ARMAND

"Hello?" I answered my phone, voice low.

"Daniels?" Nathan Moore piped.

"Yeah, you dialed my number, didn't you?"

"Yes, but you sound...I don't know, calm, and why are you whispering? Where are you?"

I rolled my eyes. "First of all, why you acting like I'm never calm?"

"No comment."

Chuckling, I continued, "I'm sitting in the waiting room at the therapist's office like a good little Cyclone."

"Oh! Okay, good."

"Why you sounding shocked? Isn't this a requirement for me being on the team? Didn't you negotiate this as a part of my contract?"

"I did, I'm just...surprised *and* proud. You don't have a history of complying."

"But noncompliance would be...counterintuitive, correct?"

No reply from Nathan, so I asked, "You still there, Nate?"

"Yeah, and whoever you are, can you put my client on the phone? I mean, I still can't believe you didn't get in a fight during or after the Bulls game."

"Again, that would've been counterintuitive."

"Wow," Nathan said.

"Mr. Daniels." That was Mr. Charles summoning me, so I told Nate, "Gotta go. My therapist is calling me."

"Okay, tell him I'ma see about getting him a bonus, because shit!" Nate quipped.

Ending the call, I was smiling as I headed into the inner office.

ELLA

Wow, so she missed One's memorial and went to a Cyclones game?

He loved her so much. How could she disrespect him like this?!

Damn, I thought they were #relationshipgoals for real. I can't believe she'd do him like this. He ain't even been dead that long.

I guess watching her old ass uncle play ball was more important than paying honor to her man.

I'm so disappointed. I loved On One. I would still be devastated if I were her.

Fuck Ella McClain! Dude loved her. RIP On One.

I'm not surprised. I never liked her stuck-up ass anyway. Bitch.

And on and on the comments went under a post on the Tea Steepers' IG page. It was a photo of me taken during the last Cyclones home game. The caption read: *Ella McClain misses On One's memorial service to attend her uncle's game.*

I wish I could say I was surprised at the reactions, but I wasn't. All the romanticized posts I'd been tagged in over the past two years told me people hadn't let their idea of what we had go, and I honestly understood why. We were always in the spotlight. There was even a limited reality show called *One and Ella* which I regretted agreeing to being a part of. So it made sense that they'd think I hadn't let go either, but I had. It was imperative that I let go and forgive both him and me. I *had* to move on. I had to live.

My phone rang, and I prayed it wasn't my agent again. She was a sweet person and I hated to keep ignoring her calls, but I wasn't trying to discuss how we could clean up this PR mess. I didn't want to be castigated about possibly ruining my chances to work with high profile artists in the fashion industry. I just didn't care enough about all that to be concerned about it. Plus, I'd already fielded phone calls from my dad, uncles, and aunt. They were all showing their support, but the constant interaction was exhausting. I couldn't even appreciate the fans of mine who were defending me on social media.

Thankfully, it wasn't my agent. It was my stepmom, Jo. So of course I answered her.

"Hello?" I breathed into the phone.

"Hey, Ella. Uh...how are you?"

"I'm..." I sighed.

"I know. You *know* I know, but it'll get better. People will find something else to obsess about. Just keep your head up and keep being you. You don't owe anyone anything. Not even Jackson."

I held the phone, fighting tears. Besides Carlos and Mother Erica, Jo was the only other person I'd divulged the truth of my relationship with Jackson to. Not even my daddy knew the full story.

"Thank you," I whimpered.

"You know you're welcome. I'ma let you go, but call me whenever you need to. I'll be here for you."

"I know you will," I replied.

Just as we ended the call, my mother's name popped up on the screen of my phone. There was no way in heaven or hell I was answering that call.

ARMAND

I was staring down at my phone, nervous as shit, which was weird. I never got nervous about stuff like this, but also, I honestly couldn't remember the last time I *did* something like this. I hadn't had to in a long time, not since I was drafted into the league. But this woman was just...different. So I took a deep breath and hit send on the text message.

Me: *Hey.*

She replied about a minute later: *Hey.*

I was so relieved that she answered; I started grinning.

Me: *How've you been?*

Her: *Good. You wanna take me out on a date?*

Damn, she didn't even give me a chance to ask. The fuck?

Me: *Yeah.*

Her: *I heard of this club we can go to. There's a private entrance and the VIP rooms are supposed to be top tier. It's called Plush-St. Louis. They just remodeled it.*

I stared at her message before replying with: *Yeah, I know the place. So you've been thinking about us going on a date?*

Her: *I've been thinking about us doing a lot of stuff. You know you have to reserve the VIP rooms, right? Let me know when we're going.*

With a dick as hard as a master's level Organic Chemistry class, I responded with *I will.*

TWELVE

ELLA

My face was beat, hair laid, body right in a crisp white oxford shirt dress and thigh high black leather boots. The dress was unbuttoned at the neck and chest to reveal layers of gold chains. A houndstooth clutch and oversized gold hoop earrings completed the look.

Seated in my living room waiting for Armand Daniels to pick me up for our date, I felt a little anxious. I hadn't really looked at another man sexually since Jackson's death, too busy fighting demons and piecing my life back together for the mere idea to enter my mind. Now? Now I was about to go on a date with the bad boy of the NBA. I guess I had a thing for bad boys, even if I was the only person privy to their badness.

I'd texted him my address in reply to his message indicating the day and time of this little date, even sent directions, and hoped he wouldn't be late because I couldn't stand tardiness.

My anxiousness morphed into excitement when my gate called my phone indicating that the code had been entered. I pressed the pound key to open the gate and waited. Moments later, a knock sounded at my door, and a smile popped up on my face as I moved to answer it. Armand was fine as hell standing there in jeans and a bright orange t-shirt with some anime character on it. A huge diamond stud in his left ear and a crazy pair of vintage Nike Waffle Trainers completed his look. I liked his style.

"Hey," I greeted him, "I see you found the place."

Deep dimples accented his smile as he said, "Yeah. You gave good directions. You look good."

"Thank you. So do you," I replied, looking him up and down again.

Somehow, that gorgeous smile of his widened. "Thanks, Miss McClain. You ready?" he asked, proffering me an enormous hand.

Sliding my clutch under my arm while taking his warm hand, I said, "Yes."

ARMAND

She slipped her little purse under her arm and took my hand, stopping to set her security system and lock her front door before letting me lead her to my vehicle parked on her stone driveway. Her mouth dropped open as we approached it.

"Is this new?" she asked as I opened the passenger door for her. "I thought you drove an Urus."

"I do. Got this for our date," I replied, shutting her door.

As I slid behind the wheel, I could hear her say, "This is a Cullinan."

Grinning, I nodded as I looked over at her.

"You bought a Cullinan just for this date?"

"Not *just* for the date, e*specially* for the date. Buckle up, Miss McClain."

She did, and we made most of the ride to *Plush* in silence

except for the music filling the inside of the truck—one of the playlists from my phone.

Once we arrived at our destination, Ella slid on a pair of sunglasses, and I smiled. "You going full incognigga, huh? Ain't tryna be seen with me?" I asked, not that I could blame her.

She shook her head. "I don't...I'm over people being in my business."

"Even your family?"

"Even them."

"I feel you on that. Let me call the manager. He's supposed to meet us and escort us inside."

She nodded her response.

PLUSH WAS ALWAYS a nice joint but the renovations had sent it over the top. That plus the fact that they'd built private rooms for VIP to replace the previous open floor concept had transformed the place from a mere nightclub to a night life experience in pure luxury.

In a word, it was lit!

A soft white sectional, a floor-to-ceiling glass wall providing a view of the dance floor, a private bar with bartender, an ensuite restroom, a crazy speaker system piping in the DJ's set—as far as I could see, it was well worth the money I'd coughed up.

"If you need anything, let Frankie, your bartender, know, and he'll get word to me," Elias, the manager, advised us.

"Can Frankie leave?" Ella asked.

I just looked at her with wide eyes. So she wanted privacy? *Hell* yeah!

Elias observed me as if waiting for my confirmation, so I said, "If she don't want him here, neither do I."

He nodded. "Very well. You have my number. Call me if you need anything."

After he and Frankie left, Ella walked over to the glass wall, watching the activity below. I wasn't sure what to do. Now that I was in a room alone with her, I felt like a kid, all nervous and shit. Yeah, I was kind of famous, even if it was for being troubled. Yeah, I had money and access to anything I could dream of wanting. Yes, I'd had women, *many* women, but this was *Ella McClain*, hands down one of the most beautiful women in the entire world. She'd grown up rich, had traveled the world, and was once the girlfriend of a huge rap star. Never mind that her dad was a legend and her mother had always been fine as hell. I was in a room alone with fucking royalty. I needed a drink.

So I made myself one—a shot of Hennessy Pure White that I quickly threw back. After glancing at her still standing at the window wall, chocolate thighs peeking out the tops of those boots, I took another shot.

"You planning on getting drunk or you planning on getting to know me?" she asked in an Americanized version of her mom's voice. She'd removed her sunglasses, and her eyelids were low as she smiled at me over her shoulder.

In response, I left the bar, finding a seat on the sectional. "I'm all about you, Miss McClain. You gon' come sit with me?"

She glided toward the sofa, sitting mere inches to my right, the perfume that had me damn near woozy in my truck following her. Turning her head, she locked eyes with me before giving me a smile. "Are you nervous to be here with me, Armand?"

I shrugged. "Maybe a little."

"Why?"

I wanted to lie. Shit, I probably *should have* lied, but something about this woman made honesty more appealing to me. "Because I've had a crush on you for a minute. It's crazy being here with you."

Her thick lashes dropped and lifted as she twisted her mouth to the side. "A crush? I'm flattered. After all, I know the girls are after you. You're virtually everyone's #mancrusheveryday."

Grinning, I shrugged again. "Everybody loves a bad boy."

"Hmmm."

"That why you're here with me right now? You like bad boys?"

"That might have something to do with it. I mean, I do like a challenge."

"A challenge? I ain't no challenge. Not when it comes to you."

Damn, what was I saying?

Her eyebrows lifted. "Oh, really?"

Licking my lips, I nodded. "Yeah."

Her eyes were locked on my mouth now, which made me focus on hers—full, soft-looking, juicy.

Without a word, she reached over and touch my top lip, her eyes never leaving my mouth as her finger moved to my bottom lip. Then she shifted toward me, kicking a leg over my thighs and straddling me. Instinct made me grab her hips as her mouth hovered over mine. I stared at her, her eyes still on my mouth as she lowered her face, pressing her lips to my mouth, licking my mouth. In seconds, we were tasting each other's tongues in a kiss so damn sloppy and hectic that I swear I got lost, time stopped, and I forgot how to breathe. She felt so soft against me, the weight of her long body felt so right, and the flavor of her kisses was like nothing I'd ever tasted before.

We kissed and kissed and kissed, my hand sliding up and down her back, meeting her ass at one point. Her bare ass. I gasped into her mouth as she reached behind herself, grabbing my wrist and moving my hand between us, to her pussy.

Her *naked* pussy.

Ella-motherfucking-McClain was in my got damn lap with no panties on!

Commando like a motherfucker!

My dick took this as a sign to act up, and I guess she liked that, because the next thing I knew, she was rolling her hips, sliding that naked pussy of hers over my hardness through my pants.

That's when I ended the kiss, throwing my head back while trying not to completely lose my shit. When I felt her lips, then her teeth, on my neck, I lifted my head to kiss her again. She moaned into my mouth, rolling her hips faster and faster and faster, and then she...stopped. She just stopped moving, sliding off my lap and leaving me with a rock-hard dick and a lonely mouth.

I watched as she stood from the sofa, pulling that dress down. "I'll be right back," she said, grabbing her purse from the sofa and heading into the restroom.

There I sat, intensely horny and wildly confused. None of that improved when she emerged from the restroom and informed me that she was ready to leave, but what could I do other than drive her home? So I did. She didn't utter another word between the club and her house other than, "Thank you," once I'd walked her to her door.

This woman was strange, weird as shit, but I still wanted her.

Now that I'd tasted her kisses and smelled her essence, I wanted her more than ever before.

THIRTEEN

ELLA

It took me three days to pull myself together. Things like what happened at *Plush* with Armand didn't happen to me. I didn't let my damn hormones rule me. I liked being in control and I liked being in control at all times. It was a necessary skill I'd picked up after Jackson's death because I believed our situation wouldn't have gone so far off the rails if I hadn't let it. That part was clearly my fault. It was an error I never planned on repeating, but Armand? Those lips, that tongue, the way he smelled, the way his body felt against and underneath mine, the fact that this big, powerful, mean-as-hell man was visibly nervous in my presence? All of that made me lose myself in the moment, in...*him*, and I was barely able to rein myself in.

Barely.

So, three days passed before I reached out to him. Three days of me trying to convince myself that Armand Daniels would not be my undoing. I still wasn't one hundred percent positive that was true when I finally contacted him.

Me: *Can we talk?*

A whole five minutes later he replied with: *About what?*

I sighed.

Me: *I'm sorry.*

Him: *About what?*

Me: *Come to my house and I'll elaborate.*

No response from him so I added: *Please.*

Him: *When?*

THIS MAN WAS RIDICULOUSLY FINE.

Always.

Like, every time I had the pleasure of seeing him, he was just... fine! This time, he wore black sweatpants and a black hoodie with gold lettering that read, "BLACKNIFICENT." His expression was serious but not hostile. I kind of wanted it to be hostile. After all, I *did* like a challenge.

Smiling, I leaned against the front doorframe and greeted him with, "Hi."

Crossing his powerful arms over his chest, he gave me a rather terse, "Hi," in return.

I was still smiling when I asked, "You're mad at me?"

"Why would I be mad at you?"

"Come on in and let me explain myself."

He did, following me to my bar-height kitchen table, taking a seat on one of the stools. I could feel his eyes on me as I took a seat across from him in my robe and slippers.

Licking his lips, he asked, "So...what's up? Why you do that the other night?"

"Can you not do that? It's distracting," I countered.

With a frown, he said, "You invite me over here to talk but I can't ask questions? The fuck are you on?"

"No, I meant the licking your lips thing. Can you not do that?"

A smile crept up on his face, a devious one. Then he licked his lips again. "Oh, okay."

I rolled my eyes and told myself not to move, not to climb in his lap and rub myself all over him. "Anyway," I resumed, "I want to apologize if it appeared that I was sending mixed signals the other night. I...like you. I want you, but I want you on my terms."

"You started it, so wasn't it on your terms?" he asked, leaning forward with his arms on the table.

"Yes and no. I...I'll be right back," I said, leaving him in the kitchen as I headed to my bedroom, quickly returning with a stack of papers.

"These are my terms," I informed him, handing him the papers.

FOURTEEN

ARMAND

"What the fuck is this?" I asked, my eyebrows wrinkled up to be damned.

"A contract," she said, her face blank. "You know...a confidential agreement."

"I can see that, but *what the fuck is this?*" I reiterated. "What is a Dominant/submissive Contract? You want me to tie you up? We don't need a contract for that. I'll tie you up, tie you down, whatever."

On God I would.

In a second.

Hell, in less than a second.

Right then and there.

On sight.

"No," she said through a sigh. I think this was the first time I'd seen her without makeup.

Beautiful.

And *still* confusing as hell.

"No?" I replied. "No what?"

"No, I don't want *you* to tie *me* up. *I* want to tie *you* up... among other things."

What in the whole fuck?

I sat there for a moment before I started laughing—doubled over, holding my stomach, tears in my eyes, laughing because she wanted to do what?

Hell naw! She couldn't be serious.

When I finally got myself together, I looked up to see her staring at me, face blank again.

"So...you wanna dominate me, Miss McClain? On One let you do that to him?" I asked.

Her eyes narrowed. "The first thing you need to know is that he's not up for discussion. *Ever*. That's a deal breaker, just like this contract. You wanna fuck me? Then trust and believe I'm very serious about being the Dominant one in this relationship."

Relationship? I liked the sound of that. "Okay...so let's say I sign this contract—"

"You have to fill it out first. We have to fill it out together."

"Okay, let's say we fill it out and sign it and everything; then what? I get to fuck you?"

"If and when I choose to let you, yes."

Here's the thing, I was just about willing to swallow fire to get in between her legs, so why not? I'd play along, sign her little contract, whatever. As serious as she was acting, wasn't no way she actually thought I was going to let her dominate me.

No way.

"All right. Let's do this," I said, watching as she visibly relaxed as if she was relieved. I had to fight not to smile.

"Okay, fill out the top with your name and age where it says sub, and then read over our roles listed in the next section," she said.

"My age?"

"Just making sure you're old enough to consent."

"I'm twenty-eight, pretty sure I'm older than you."

"Then put twenty-eight on the paper."

I did, more or less scanning over our roles like:

Dom will keep sub safe.

Dom will provide a safe space for sub.

Dom is responsible for properly training sub on how to please her.

Dom will have unrestricted use of sub's body.

Stuff like that.

Some of the sub role stuff was wild, though, like the sub was basically supposed to be at the Dom's total disposal, under their complete control.

The sub will research and learn about BDSM.

The sub's body belongs to the Dom.

The sub will submit to the Dom at all times, and then—

"I ain't supposed to fuck nobody else? So...what? This supposed to be a *relationship* relationship?" I asked.

She nodded. "That's non-negotiable. You can't have sex with anyone else as long as we are in this...arrangement. You also can't masturbate."

"What?!"

She stared at me.

"My bad. I ain't mean to yell. So...you must be planning on giving me a lot of pussy. Like *a whole lot*."

"That and you're going to have to learn some self-control."

"You saying I don't have self-control?"

"You saying you do?"

Damn.

"Uh...I don't know if I can do that. The not masturbating part, I mean. That's one of my favorite pastimes, and how you gonna know if I do?" I challenged.

"I'll know," she countered. "And when I know, you'll be punished accordingly."

I grinned, leaning across the table while licking my lips. "What you gon' do? Spank me?"

She leaned forward, too, her face only inches from mine. "Is that what you want me to do? I'm good at it."

"This bad bitch energy you're giving off? It's got my dick hard," I admitted.

"Too bad you can't do anything about it until I allow you to. Now, you need to choose a safe word. A safe word is—"

"I know what that is. I saw *Fifty Shades of Grey*."

"Really?" she screeched.

"Yeah. Damn! I watch movies and shit."

"A woman made you watch it, huh?" she said with a smirk.

"Ain't nobody made me do *shit*," I shot back. Alyssa Howard didn't *make* me watch it. I just watched it and acted like I enjoyed it so I could get some pussy. There's a difference.

Lifting her hands, she said, "Touché. So, you need time to think of one?"

"Nah. I got one."

"Okay..."

"Uh...personal. Like the foul."

She nodded. "Personal it is. What are your hard limits, things that you absolutely will not agree to doing or having done to you?"

"Basically, my whole ass region is off limits. Don't do nothing to my ass. That's a hard limit like a motherfucker."

She smiled. "Fair enough, although I think you'd enjoy having your prostate massaged."

This time, *I* stared at *her*.

Shrugging, she said, "Your loss. So you're down for everything else? Flogging, rope play, wax play, edging, paddling—"

I was only half listening but said, "Yeah, I'm good with everything else."

"Wonderful!" she gushed.

This was some weird shit, but if the end product was me being inside her, I was going to roll with it.

"The last thing I need you to do is list your favorite foods, movies, TV shows, hobbies, and materials like fur, silk, cotton. Then we can sign off on everything."

"And then?" I asked.

"And then, I need to see STD results for you. Recent ones. I'll give you mine, and after that, we can schedule our first play date. We'll work around your schedule. I'm pretty flexible. I don't have any work lined up for a couple months."

"Big model shit, huh?"

"Yeah. Oh! And I have an IUD, so no need for condoms as long as you're clean. I can provide you with proof of that, too."

I nodded. "Bet."

I'd finished filling out the contract while she watched me and was about to sign it when she grabbed my hand. "Are you sure you don't have any other hard limits? There's nothing else you don't want me to do to you or...at all?" she asked.

I looked up and into her eyes as she stared into mine. We sat like that for more than a minute before I said, "You can't fuck anyone else, either."

This time *she* nodded. "Okay."

ELLA

"I don't want to do another reality show. I loved it when I was a kid, but I've spent most of my life being followed by cameras. I just want some normalcy now," I said, my face focused on the ceiling. It was so like him to do this, to wait until after we'd had some great sex to spring this on me.

"Damn, you acting like I'm asking you to cut your leg off or something. This show is a big deal for me, El! The network won't sign off on it if you don't agree to be a part of it, and how it's gonna look anyway for me to have a show and you not be a part of it? Damn! You always do this!" he thundered, making me flinch. "How you gon' want normalcy and be with a famous nigga at the same time? Don't make no sense!"

He could be so...scary sometimes. Not violent, per se, just... unstable. I was more fearful of him hurting himself than anyone else.

"I always do what? When have I ever refused you anything? I'm here now because you want me here instead of my apartment in Houston studying for midterms!"

"So you didn't want to come? You don't want to be with me?"

"I didn't say that, Jackson! It just would've made more sense for you to come to me."

"You know I couldn't!"

"I know that's what you said..."

"So I'm lying? You know what? Fuck this!"

He snatched the covers off his body and left the bed without bothering to turn the light on. In the darkness, I could hear him getting dressed. I also heard the familiar sounds of pills rattling in a bottle and keys jingling. Then I heard him leave the bedroom. A few moments later, I heard the front door to his condo slam shut.

I closed my eyes and sighed before grabbing my phone and dialing his number.

"What?!" was how he answered my call.

"Jackson, come back. You shouldn't be out driving this late while you're upset. We can talk about this, come to some kind of agreement."

"An agreement? You really think you're better than me, don't you?"

"What? No! You know I'm not like that!"

"I know I ain't got a rich daddy, Ella. I ain't got a famous mama. I ain't grow up with shit! I built everything I got and I'm tryna share it with you. I'm just asking for a little help! This is for us, for our future!"

I felt the beginnings of a headache and was wearing a nearly permanent look of confusion on my face. "Jackson—"

"Don't worry about it. I'm used to this. I don't need you to do *shit* for me." His words were garbled, like he had something in his mouth.

My heart stuttered. "Please don't do this. Where are you? How many pills did you take?"

"I ain't take enough to deal with your bullshit."

"Where are you?!" I screamed, a panic rising inside me.

"In the car. In the parking deck."

I was on my feet, half-dressed at that point. "Stay there."

I left the condo, finding him just where he said he was. I was so young at the time—just nineteen years old—and inexperienced that I ran to him, dove headfirst into his toxic behavior and an ill-fitting caregiver role, climbed into that car, looked him right in his heavy-lidded eyes, and agreed to do the show.

That memory, one of many that haunted me from time to time, was triggered by the sound of the bottle of pain killers shifting in my bedside table drawer when I opened it. Although these were over the counter and not the Percocet Jackson kept in stock, they still reminded me of just how traumatic my time with him was, how with each passing day, our romance seemed to veer farther and farther off its intended path until it crashed in the worst way.

I stared at that bottle of pain reliever for thirty minutes while sitting on the side of my bed, and when those memories became more than I could handle, I lay back in the bed, pulled the covers over my head, and cried.

I WAS FINALLY FORCED out of bed by my bladder, dragging myself to my feet and shuffling to the bathroom. I hadn't eaten or drunk anything all day, and I recognized that I was on my way to a full-on depressive episode, something I was familiar with but fought hard to avoid re-experiencing.

I was losing control of myself, and I didn't like it.

At all.

When my phone rang, it was a welcomed distraction because of the name that flashed across its screen.

I actually smiled when I answered it with, "Hello, Armand."

"Hey."

Frowning, I asked, "Don't you have a game?"

"I do. It's halftime and I needed to ask you something."

"Should you be on your phone during halftime?"

"No. I'm supposed to be taking a piss. Look, I was reading about BDSM like it said for me to do in the contract, and this one article said something about the Dom having a special name or title, like something the sub is supposed to call them. You got one?"

The fact that he was actually doing his homework made my nipples harden. "Yes," I said, taking a second to think before informing him, "Sir. You are to call me sir."

"I ain't calling you no damn sir. Fuck that."

"Hmm, we'll see."

ARMAND

We won the game, and I couldn't wait to get into something or *someone* to celebrate. Everyone was in a good mood on our bus ride back to our hotel in Memphis. Energy was high and I had to admit that I was getting kind of comfortable being a Cyclone, but not too comfortable. I'd been traded too many times to let my guard down.

Once we made it to the hotel, I was one of the last players off the bus and almost groaned when I saw McClain standing on the sidewalk looking for me.

As I approached him, he said, "Damn, man. Why you gotta look like you wanna hurl or something?"

"'Cause I do," I admitted. "What's up, man? You know I ain't tryna be your friend."

"Yeah, I know. You know your mom's birthday is coming up, right?"

"You think I don't, nigga?" I really did forget though.

"My bad. So anyway, I'm throwing her a party. Just wanted to let you know. It would make her real happy for you to be there."

"Lil' Leland and Layla gon' be there? Or y'all sending them to a sitter?"

"They'll be there until their bedtime."

As we began walking into the building, I said, "I'll be there. I mean, I live on the property anyway."

"Good. Good. I'll get the details to you."

I WAS STEPPING out the shower in my room when I heard the phone ring and almost missed her call, so my "hello" made me sound like I was running.

"Armand?" she said.

"Yeah, it's me. I was rushing, tryna get to the phone."

"Well, I was just calling to remind you of the no sex rule."

"I got it. Damn!"

"That includes blowjobs from random groupies."

Fuck.

"Yeah...I figured that," I said, but I really thought that was a loophole.

"I bet you did. Also, as soon as you get off the plane tomorrow, come to my house."

"Why?"

"Because I said so, and if you keep questioning me, you can expect to be punished. I can think of worse things than just flogging you. *Way* worse."

She hung up, and I was left standing there holding my phone thinking, *damn.*

FIFTEEN

ELLA

The first thing I noticed when I opened the door for him was his scent, a mixture of soap, cologne...and him.

"You didn't come directly here from the airport, did you?" I asked.

"What?" he replied, his pretty hazel eyes narrowed at me.

"You went home and showered."

"Well, yeah. I figured you ain't want me funky."

Backing out of the doorway, I said, "Come in."

He did, trailing me through my house as he inquired, "You always walk around in robes? You don't never get dressed when you're here?"

I didn't answer as I led him into my bedroom.

"This your room? It fits. Real princess-like," he observed.

"Mmhmm," I said, stopping at the foot of my bed, turning to face him, and dropping my robe.

"Oh my god," he muttered, his eyes sliding up and down my exposed body. "Shit!"

"When we're about to play—"

"Like do a scene?" he interrupted me.

I smiled. "Yes, that. The first thing you need to do is get naked and assume the position."

"Okay," he said slowly.

Then he just stood there staring at me, so I said, "Take your clothes off, Armand."

"Oh, you mean like now? I gotcha."

I watched as he shucked his clothes, my breath catching in my throat once his full nakedness was revealed. His body—tall and muscular and chiseled—was...I don't know, but I knew I had never seen anything so beautiful in all my life. Unable to help myself, I moved closer for a better inspection. I was tall, too, six feet, so he didn't exactly tower over me, but the look in his stormy eyes, the rigidness of his guarded posture, the length and girth of his hard dick? They all screamed hazard, and that made my mouth water.

Pulling myself together, I said, "After you take your clothes off, I want you on your knees."

"You want what? Like doggystyle on my knees? Ain't no way. Fuck that."

I moved even closer to him, grabbing one of his nipples and tweaking it. He moaned a little and I smiled. "You want this pussy. I can smell the desire on you. If you're a good boy and obey me, you just might get it. Now, on your *fucking* knees."

He dropped like a basketball onto all fours, and I said, "Good boy." Backing away from him, I added, "You have no idea how beautiful you look right now."

He grunted in response.

Sliding my red stiletto fingernails over the bronze skin covering his back, I said, "Sit up on your knees and put your hands behind your back. Head down."

Surprisingly, he quickly did as he was told, but I could feel his eyes on me as I walked to my bedside table, returning to him with a pair of solid gold handcuffs. Holding them up, I said, "Only the best for you."

His eyes were wide as I stepped behind him and clicked the handcuffs in place around his wrists. Then I sauntered around him, moving so close that my naked mound was mere inches from his face.

"Damn," he groaned.

"You wanna touch it?" I asked.

"Hell yeah," he admitted. "I wanna touch it, lick it, fuck it. Shit, you smell good."

"Thank you, but you forgot something."

"What? What else can you do to a pussy?"

"You forgot to call me sir."

"I told you I ain't—"

I interrupted him by pressing my hairy mound against his face.

His, "Got damn!" was muffled.

"Got damn what?"

Nothing from him, so I grabbed the back of his head, pressing it against my pussy. He groaned like he was dying, but still, no *sir*. He was forcing me to bring out the heavy artillery. So I backed away from him, watching as he gasped and looked up at me, pupils dilated.

When I dropped to my knees before him, I heard him mutter, "My god."

I lowered myself until I was face to face with his perfectly veined dick, hiking my ass up in the air as I flicked my tongue across the head of his erection.

"Shit!" he murmured.

"Shit, what?" I asked.

Silence from Armand.

I took him deep in my mouth and popped him out.

"Ohhhh, fuck!" he yelled.

"Oh, fuck what?"

"I...ain't...calling...you...sir," he hissed, voice strained.

"Oh, you're not?"

I lifted my body, coming face to face with him, licking his lips before kissing him. When he opened his mouth for me, I bit his tongue before dropping back down to take him in my mouth again. This time, I sucked and sucked and sucked until I could feel his body begin to tremble. That's when I stopped, standing to my feet and staring down at him. His eyes were closed, chest heaving, Adam's apple bobbing up and down as he swallowed.

"El...Ella, I—"

"*Sir*. You will refer to me as *sir*."

He shook his head. I, in turn, nodded before dropping to my knees again, ass in the air as I did my best to swallow him whole, gagging loudly.

"Shit. Shit, shit, shit," he uttered, breathing ragged.

Reaching up, I tweaked his nipple, popped him out of my mouth, and left the room.

Standing just outside the bedroom doorway, I watched him, still in position, his back to me as he moved his wrists and mumbled something I couldn't make out. He was probably cursing me out. That thought made me smile.

When I returned, I stood before him with my legs wide open. "It's not enough for you to read about BDSM. The purpose of you studying was for you to understand your role, but I suppose you can't understand what I don't teach you. So I've been being lenient with you. You disobeyed me by going home before coming here. I told you to keep your head down when you're in this position, but you're staring at me right now. You refuse to call me sir and you keep fucking talking." I moved to press my mound to his face, which was still not lowered. "In this space, I have the control, *all* of the control. You speak when I give you permission to. You look at me when I give you permission to. You touch me when I allow it. You don't even cum unless I let you, and you *fucking call me sir*!"

Back on my knees, I licked the head of his dick again. "See, you think this is a joke, but I assure you this is very serious."

He gasped as I took him in my mouth again, sucking until I felt him shudder. Then I stopped, leaving the room again. This went on for so long that a sheen of sweat covered his body and he literally began babbling incoherently. He wanted to cum. At that point he *needed* to, but would I let him? I wasn't sure. One thing about it, he never looked as attractive to me as he did in that moment—big, powerful, and completely vulnerable.

Returning to him for probably the fifteenth time, I asked, "Do you want me to let you cum, Armand?"

He didn't reply, so I added, "You may speak."

"Yes...*please*," he croaked.

"Yes please what?" I said through my teeth.

"Yes...please...sir."

Pride blossomed in my chest as I dropped to the floor and sucked his dick until he screamed my name as his seed shot down my throat.

ARMAND

She took the cuffs off me, and my arms dropped to my sides; then I heard her say, "Stand up. I'll help you."

I felt...mindless, numb in the best way. Like, I felt nothing and everything all at once. I was stiff as hell as I stood, my eyes closed as I tried to catch my breath. My heart was doing the electric slide. My legs felt heavy.

"Sit here. Drink this," she ordered, placing a bottle of water in my hand.

Where did that come from? I wondered. Nevertheless, I chugged the water because I was parched as hell.

She left me sitting at the foot of her pink bed, and my eyes dropped to my feet as I dug my toes into the soft pink rug. I'm not sure how long I sat there like that before she came back, taking my hand.

"Come on, baby," she said.

I nodded, letting her lead me into her bathroom to a huge bathtub.

"Get in," she instructed.

And I did, sinking into the hot water with a groan. A few seconds later, she was in the tub too, standing over me, her eyes glued to me as she said, "Scoot forward so I can sit behind you."

I nodded, moved, and was soon sitting with my back against her soft body.

She took a washcloth and squeezed water over my chest, my shoulders, my arms, as she softly asked, "How do you feel?"

"I can speak?" I asked.

"If I ask you a question, yes."

"I don't know how I feel other than tired."

"Then relax. We can stay in here as long as you want. Then you have to eat, and if you want, we can take a nap together or watch TV."

"Word? This that aftercare shit, huh?"

"Mmhmm. How do your wrists feel?"

"Sore."

"That's because you were fighting against the cuffs. You can't do that."

"I couldn't help it. I...I wanted to touch you."

"And I might let you...eventually. Do you bruise easily?"

"Nah. I mean...no, sir. I don't think so."

"Very good. I have some cream I'll rub on your wrists just in case."

"Okay...sir."

. . .

I WOKE up to darkness and an empty bed. I remembered falling asleep with her body wrapped around mine, but now she was gone, and I kind of panicked, sitting up, my breathing loud in my own ears. I wanted to call her name but wasn't sure if that was allowed, but then I thought if the punishment was going to be her sucking my dick until I entered another plane of consciousness, then fuck it.

"Ella! Uh...sir?!"

Nothing.

I left the bed, noticing that the bathroom door was closed. I knocked on it and in a softer voice said, "Sir, you in there?"

Her "yes" was quiet, shaky. "I'll be out in a moment."

"Okay. Uh...sir."

I climbed back in the bed and waited. When she finally rejoined me, pressing her body against mine, I involuntarily let out a moan.

"How do you feel now? You hungry? I could make more tacos," she said.

Tacos were my favorite. Now I understood what the list of my likes was for. "I feel...good, and I'm not hungry. It's late. You want me to leave, sir?"

After a long moment of silence, she whispered, "No."

SIXTEEN

ARMAND

Sitting at her kitchen table the next morning while she cooked breakfast, I wasn't sure what to do. I kept my eyes on the screen of my almost dead phone and tried not to cum from the memory of her mouth on me yesterday. That shit? That shit was some earth-shaking, life-changing kind of goodness.

Damn!

My brain was back at maximum performance, the floating numb feeling gone, and I can admit that I missed it.

A plate appeared before me on the table—soft-cooked bacon and toast with butter, sugar, and jelly. I smiled as I said, "Permission to speak, sir?"

"You may speak, and you may lift your head."

I looked up, meeting her gaze. "Thank you, sir."

"You're welcome. Eat up," she said as she sat across from me with her own plate of food.

. . .

ABOUT THIRTY MINUTES LATER, I was heading out her front door when her voice stopped me. "Go straight home, and FaceTime me when you get there."

"Why?" I asked.

She stared at me with one raised eyebrow.

"Um...I meant to say...yes, sir."

She kissed my cheek and I left. When I made it home, I FaceTimed her, informing her, "I'm here." I was still tired and more than ready to climb in my bed.

"Good. Now come back," she ordered.

"Come back where?"

"Where do you think? Where did you just leave from?"

"I...you want me to come back now?"

In response, she did that staring thing.

So I said, "Yes, sir," walked back out my little home, got in my truck, and drove to her house.

When she let me in, the expression on her face told me all I needed to know. Without a word, I undressed right in her living room and lowered myself to my knees, fixing my eyes on the floor.

ELLA

I wondered if he had any idea how powerful he was in his submission, how I nearly came undone just from seeing this vision of him. Broad shoulders, perfect body, big hands, all sheathed in warm brown skin. He wasn't only powerful; he was majestic with his head lowered as if awaiting placement of his crown—*breathtaking*.

"Good boy," I crooned as I stood over him, threading my fingers through his short dreadlocks. I rounded him, squatting behind him to kiss his bare back, causing him to flinch from the unexpected contact. "You are...so damn fine. You know that?"

"Yes, sir," he answered.

"Other women have told you that?"

"Yes, sir."

"A lot of other women?"

"Yes, sir."

"Hmmm, do you think of those other women often?"

"Not anymore. I just think of you, sir."

I smirked. "You catch on fast. Good answer."

"It's the truth, sir."

"I bet it is."

ARMAND

I was on my back in her bed, wrists and ankles tied to the bed posts with soft rope and a pretty pussy hovering over me. She was squatting over my face as she held onto the headboard and talked shit to me.

"You like this pussy, Armand?" she asked, voice low and husky.

"Yes, sir," I groaned.

"What do you like about it?"

"It's-it's pretty and it smells so good."

"Does it? You see how wet it is?"

"Y-yes, sir. It's real wet."

"You wanna touch it?"

"Oh, hell yeah...sir! Shit!"

"You like to eat pussy, Armand?"

"I'd like to eat *your* pussy, sir. I wanna eat it *bad*."

"I just might let you, but for now..."

Her pussy left my view as she moved from above me, and then she said, "I'm going to cover your eyes."

"Uh...okay, sir."

She lifted my head, slipping a black blindfold over my eyes. Out of nowhere. I heard music—something slow and bass-heavy. Whatever it was sounded nice and sexy. It was definitely a vibe.

I lay there for what felt like forever, immobile, blind to my surroundings, and hard as a brick before I felt the bed dip between my legs and her hands on my thighs. Next, I felt her slide down me, cocooning my dick in a pussy so wet and hot and tight that tears sprung into my eyes.

I gasped as she lifted up and slid back down.

"Damn," she muttered, placing her hands on my chest and kissing my neck, cheeks, and mouth as she rode me. "You feel good, Armand."

My mouth dropped open as I jerked my hands, forgetting they were bound. I wanted to touch her so damn bad!

"Stop fighting the ropes, Armand."

I nodded. "Yes...sirrrrr!" I howled.

She stopped, lifting from me and taking her good-ass pussy with her.

Fuck!

My distress left when I felt the warmth of her mouth on me. My ass sank deeper into the mattress as I involuntarily moaned.

"P-permission to speak, sir?" I managed to say.

She let me slide out of her mouth and said, "Speak."

"Okay...you got some good pussy, sir!"

"Thank you. Better than my head game?"

"No, sir...they're equally good."

With her mouth on me again, she hummed, "Mmhmm."

She sucked and gagged and slurped for a good minute before she stopped, replacing her mouth with her magical pussy and making me whimper, "Oh got damn!"

She kissed me, sharing the taste of her pussy combined with the flavor of my dick, and when she took her mouth from mine, I whined, "I'ma c-c-cum!"

"Not until I say you can, and—" She tweaked my nipple, *hard.* "—you forgot to say sir. Forget again and I won't let you talk at all while I'm riding this dick. No talking, no moaning, *nothing.*"

"Shit! Fuck! Got damn! I'ma cum, sir!"

She lifted up and slammed back down, grunting, "You better the-fuck not!"

"Ohhhhhh, I can't hold it. I can't—"

She was gone again, and I lay there breathing hard, chest heaving, toes tingling. "Sir...sir..." I mumbled.

"You've got to learn to hold it," she said. "The longer you hold it, the better the release will feel."

"Shit, I'm trying, sir. I...help me!"

"I am," she said, and then...silence. Nothing from her and nothing from me for a good minute until I felt the bed shift and smelled her unique musk right above my nose. Before I could think through what was happening, her pussy was on my face, and my knee-jerk reaction was to lick it. I licked and licked and sucked and sucked and moaned and whimpered and licked and sucked some more as she rode my face and sang my name. She tasted good, sweet, perfect.

I *loved* this shit.

My dick was still hard but the only thing on my mind was getting her off, and as her ride grew wilder and wilder, I knew I was getting the job done. Then she stiffened, her hands gripping my head. Things had gotten so chaotic that the blindfold had slid up enough for me to see her—head thrown back, mouth hanging open as she rode out her orgasm.

Fucking beautiful.

When she dropped her head, our eyes locked, but neither of us spoke. We stared at each other for a good while, her breathing heavily and me wanting to fill her mouth with her flavor. Finally, I asked, "Can I kiss you, sir?"

In lieu of an answer, she slid down my body, taking my dick and lining it up with her pussy. She slid down on me again, impossibly wet now. Leaning forward, she not only kissed me; she slowly licked her juices off my face and said, "Now you can cum."

I did, releasing a nut that made me scream until I nearly lost my voice.

ELLA

"Ohhhh, damn! Go, little penguin! You gon' get fucked up if you don't—aw, hell! He got him!" Armand rasped. He was giving commentary on a nature documentary as we witnessed a penguin being attacked by a seal.

"You really like these documentaries, huh? I thought it was a joke when I saw you'd listed them as one of your favorites," I said through a laugh.

"I love this shit, survival of the fittest at its best. Like, everything has its place and purpose in nature. Ain't nothing personal. It's all about staying alive, savage or not," he said.

I rubbed a hand over his head as it lay in my lap, the rest of his body stretched across my sofa. "That makes sense. Hey, you feeling okay? Your ankles, wrists? I can massage them some more."

He looked up at me and smiled. "I'm good, sir. As long as I can lay here like this, I'm good."

I lowered my head to kiss his thick lips and said, "Then I'm good, too."

SEVENTEEN

ELLA

Me: *What are you doing?*

Armand: *Getting ready to start practice. The coach just got done yelling at me. I'm five seconds from kicking his old ass.*

Me: *What happened???*

Him: *I missed practice yesterday.*

Me: *You had practice yesterday?! Why didn't you tell me? Why would you miss it?*

Him: *Because, sir, you told me to come back. So I came back. I figured you knew I had practice and you were testing me or something.*

Me: *No! I know the game schedule, not the practice schedule. I didn't think about practice.*

Him: *I gotta go.*

Him: *I mean, I gotta go, sir.*

Me: *Okay. I need your practice schedule. Bring it to me right after you finish practice.*

Him: *Yes, sir.*

Me: *And don't fight anybody.*

He didn't reply to my last text.

"MON ANGE, how are you? I have not heard from you since you ran away from me," Claude crooned into the phone.

Tucking my right leg under me on my sofa, I replied, "I didn't run away from you. I ran away from Esther Reese. You know, the woman you ambushed me with?"

"Ella, Ella, Ella," he sighed. "Hold the line, chérie."

"Okay."

I waited for him to return to the phone and almost leapt from my seat when I heard, "Eller, darling..."

My mom. He'd ambushed me a-damn-gain!

"Wow," I scoffed, "are you sleeping with Claude now or something? That would explain why he would be willing to lose my friendship for you."

"Claude knows how much I love and miss you. He knows how much it breaks my heart that you won't talk to me. Please...just talk to me, sweetheart."

"Mom...I can't do this with you. Not now."

"Then when?"

"I don't know. Maybe never. I'm not sure I'll ever get over the things you've done."

"Ella, honey...anything I did was not to hurt *you*."

"Just my father?"

"I love your father. You know that, and I understand your allegiance to him, but don't you think I deserve the same from you as your mother?"

"A mother is supposed to be more than the person who gives birth to you. A mother is supposed to protect you and care for you! All you've done is ruin my life and you know it!"

I was near tears when I ended the call without giving her a chance to reply.

ARMAND

Candles were lit all around the living room, the location of this after-practice scene. I was in position—naked, head down, waiting for her to handcuff me or tie me to the bed or—

"Look at me," she demanded.

I did, letting my eyes inch up her flawless naked body. Ella's legs were long and shapely, her thighs rounded, her stomach flat, her breasts full, and her face...thick lips, almond-shaped eyes—pure perfection.

My already hard dick bounced as I watched her drop to a squat, the aroma of her essence drifting into my nose. Closing my eyes, I swallowed hard. I swear I could taste her pussy just by smelling it.

"I said, *look at me*," she repeated.

Opening my eyes, I found hers, and we stared at each other for more than a minute before she spoke again.

"How do you think I should punish you for not telling me about practice?" she asked.

"You could...suck my dick...sir?" I tried.

"I see I need to give you options. I can either flog you, paddle you, whip you—"

"I...it doesn't matter, sir." It really didn't as long as I got some pussy afterwards.

She stood, causing more of her scent to waft toward me. "Okay. Stand up. I'll be right back."

I stood and watched her ass as she left the room. She quickly returned with a black wooden paddle; the letters EJM were painted on it in pink. Stepping behind me, she reached a soft hand around my body and grabbed my dick, making me jump a little.

"Do you trust me?" she questioned.

"Yes...sir," I replied.

"Are you ready?"

"Yeah...you ain't gonna tie my hands up or handcuff me or nothing...sir?"

"Do you want me to? You like it when I do that?"

I hesitated before saying, "Yes, sir. I like it."

"Then no."

Before I could say anything else, something hit the back of my right thigh and I yelled, "Fuck!" She really hit me with that thing and the shit stung!

"How was that?" she asked.

"Shit...I don't know...it—"

Whack!

Another one, this time to the opposite thigh.

"Oh, damn!" I grunted.

She hit me again and again and again, alternating thighs. This was weird as hell. In the past, if I thought a motherfucker was merely *considering* hitting me, I would H-town stomp that ass, but this felt different. I mean, it hurt, but in a good way. I didn't really understand why I liked it, but I did, and when I felt her hands on the sides of my thighs and her lips on every spot the paddle had met, I gasped. *I literally gasped.* Her lips were so soft, her kisses so sweet.

I dropped my head and closed my eyes as she kissed spot after spot. Then she moved, stepping in front of me and wiping away the tears I didn't know had fallen from my eyes.

"You thought you'd hit me?" she softly asked. "That's why you wanted to be restrained?"

I nodded, my "Yes, sir," coming out low and strangled.

"But you didn't."

I nodded again, opening my eyes to see tears on her face, too, as she leaned in to kiss me, a kiss I returned so passionately that I almost fucking fainted.

When the kiss had ended, she lowered herself onto all fours and said, "Now, fuck me."

"Yes, sir."

"MR. DANIELS, how've you been since we last met?" Alvin Charles asked as if I didn't see his ass every week.

I shrugged, shifting my body on the loveseat. "A'ight...got in trouble for missing practice last week, but other than that, things have been cool."

"Missing practice? Is that a regular occurrence for you?"

"Nah, I had...uh, other obligations, but I ain't gonna do that again."

"Those other obligations must've been important..."

"It...they were. Hey, can I ask you something?"

"Sure."

"What do you think about BDSM, like for someone with my issues?"

His eyebrows flew up. "Is that something you're interested in?"

I shifted in my seat again because this was some awkward shit, but I had to talk to someone about it. Who else but him? I damn sure wasn't going to tell Scotty or any of my other friends about me being submissive, even though it was honestly lit. Ella made me feel good no matter what she did to me. "Uh...you could say that."

"Hmmm, well honestly, I *have* studied the possible therapeutic benefits of pursuing kink. My wife is also a therapist and she's done extensive research on the subject, but at any rate, it can be good for stress relief, processing emotions..."

"Yeah, what about like...dealing with aggression? I...I feel like it could help."

He stared at me for a moment. "It's likely that it could help with aggression. Armand, have you been experimenting with kink?"

I rubbed the back of my neck and blew out a breath. "I..."

He raised his hands. "You don't have to answer that, but I do want to point out that I can see a visible change in how you carry yourself just since our last session. Whatever is causing it, I'd say it benefits you."

"Yeah, I think so, too."

"YOU NEED to make time to visit the community center. You're the benefactor, you live close, and you haven't made one visit," Nate's nagging ass said.

With the speakerphone activated, I carried my cell from my bedroom to my kitchen. "You gon' find me some time to go by there? I'm working every damn day right now between games and practice." The truth was, I only bought the place for my mom, but that whole situation was something I didn't want to discuss.

"Speaking of practice..."

"I know. I know," I said before chugging some orange juice straight from the container. "Like I told Coach, it won't happen again. I apologized and everything."

"Yeah, I heard. Coach Duke said you didn't even seem that mad about being confronted. I'm...proud of you?"

I chuckled. "Man, fuck you, Nate! I *was* mad, still am. Just trying to exercise some self-control. You know?"

"Wow, um...how much is Alvin Charles charging you because I'm willing to double it. Dude is a miracle worker!"

"It ain't all him."

"Then who—wait, you met a girl? In St. Louis?"

"Yes, it's a lot of women here, you know?"

"I do know. So, you like her?"

"A lot. She's...she's different. We...I don't know. It's good, though."

"You sound kinda happy, too. Shit!"

Grinning, I admitted, "I am, but we just started messing around. I hope I don't fuck it up."

"You won't. Just be careful, man. Okay? You got a lot to protect."

"I know, but the thing is, she got money. She don't need mine."

"Good. Still, be careful, man."

"I will."

EIGHTEEN

ARMAND

"Dang, how y'all keep beating me? Y'all cheating, ain't you?" I said.

Layla and Lil' Leland both started protesting at the same time, Layla finishing with, "Nuh-uh! You just not good at basketball like us!"

"Oh, really? How am I on this game, then?" I posed. "Y'all played as me!"

"Yeah, 'cause we tryna show you how to play better!" Lil' Leland informed me.

"So y'all really think I can't play good?" I asked, fighting not to laugh. "They don't let just anybody play in the NBA, you know."

"Our daddy plays. Do your daddy play, too?" Layla asked.

I was trying to figure out how to answer that without getting in my feelings. I usually stayed out of the vicinity of a discussion regarding my sperm donor. He was a piece of shit who hit my mom and never cared enough to be my father. The easy answer would be a simple *no, he didn't play in the league*, but I couldn't even say that. My brain was capable, but my mouth wasn't getting the message, so I was thankful when Leland entered the room and broke up our little gaming session.

"All right, munchkins, your mom just pulled up. Time to join the guests in the living room."

The kids hopped up and ran out of the game room leaving me alone with their dad.

"Hey, thanks for playing with them," he said to me as we both exited the room.

"It's all good. They're cool," I stated.

"And obsessed with you. I heard Lil' Leland on his headset the other night while he was on the game bragging about his brother being Armand Daniels."

"Word?" I said with a slight frown. "He don't be bragging about you?"

"He does, but he seems more hyped about you."

"Maybe it's a brother thing. I always wanted a brother," I admitted, unsure of why it felt so easy to talk to this nigga when I still didn't like him.

"Well, now you got three...and a sister."

I stopped in my tracks, watching as he turned and walked into the living room. I stood there for so long that I almost missed my mom's entrance but made it into the room in time to scream surprise with everyone else when she entered with my cousin Zabrina. My mom was so pretty...and happy as she hugged Leland and her other kids, my...siblings?

Damn.

I just never saw them like that, as my brothers and sister, but that's what they were. I had three brothers and a sister.

When my mom spotted me, she pulled me into the tightest hug as people laughed and talked around us, saying directly into my ear, "Thank you for coming, Boogie. I love you."

Once she released me, I kissed her cheek and said, "Love you, too, Ma. Happy birthday."

She left me to greet more of the roomful of guests and I let my attention drift until it collided with her—Ella, looking edible in this tight red jumpsuit thing, her hair in braids, and standing next to her with his arm around her waist was that big buff motherfucker she brought to dinner before.

ELLA

He looked good. Angry, maybe even homicidal, but good in black slacks, a white dress shirt unbuttoned at the collar, and a Cuban link chain around his neck. His locs hung free, and his hazel eyes weren't hazel. I'd noticed that they changed colors with his mood. Tonight, they were dark, almost black. I could see that from across the room.

He was pissed off.

Completely pissed off.

I dropped my eyes as I dug in my clutch for my phone.

"Armand Daniels is heading this way," Carlos muttered, making me jerk my head up.

He was indeed on his way toward me, threading a path through the crowd of people.

"Princess, when did you get here?"

I almost jumped out of my skin at the sound of my father's voice. As he pulled me into a hug, I attempted to calm my racing heart.

"Daddy! I didn't know you were coming!" I said into his chest.

Releasing me, he gave me a peck on the forehead. "I wasn't sure we'd make it. Glad we did."

"Jo's here? The kids?"

"Jo is. The kids are with Ms. Sherry back home." He glanced around the room and added, "I don't know where Jo went."

"I'm sure I'll run into her. Where are y'all staying?" I asked.

"We got a room at the Trudeau. Don't worry, we ain't gonna crash with you. I'd love to visit with you a little, but this is a turn-around trip. We're leaving in the morning."

"Oh, okay."

He slapped hands with Carlos as he greeted him, and while they fell into a conversation, I took the opportunity to scan the room for Armand. When I located him, he was slipping out the patio doors.

"I'll be back," I said to no one in particular, heading toward the patio doors myself.

ARMAND

I smelled her first.

Even in the cool night air, her scent found me, making me close my eyes and inhale deeply. Despite the newly familiar aroma of her filling my nose, I couldn't calm myself. I couldn't get it together.

"Why you here with that dude?" No "sir" because *fuck that*. "I thought we weren't supposed to mess with other people," I growled without turning to look at her.

"We aren't and I'm not," she said, her voice calm. I could tell she'd moved closer to me.

"But you brought a fucking date? That ain't some shit you thought you needed to tell me since we got this...this arrangement going on?"

"Armand, will you turn around and look at me?" Her voice was soft, lacking the authority it usually held.

"You fucking him?"

"I already said I wasn't. He's my friend, my best friend, and he's gay."

"That nigga ain't gay."

"He's my friend. I think I'd know."

I grunted.

"Will you please turn around?"

She said please. That made me turn around.

Her eyes searched mine, her face uncharacteristically expressive as she said, "I'm sorry. I can see how it must've looked for me to show up here with Carlos."

"Carlos," I scoffed.

"Yes, *Carlos*. He popped up in town today to surprise me because...well, he was concerned about me and wanted to see me. I asked if he wanted to come here with me. If I'd known you were coming to the party, I would've told you."

I stared at her, at those eyes that always seemed to look through me to see what I needed when I needed it. Then I let my gaze travel down to her mouth.

Her mouth.

Shit, the thought of it alone had my dick standing at attention, so I grabbed the back of her neck and pulled her closer, taking her mouth in a rough kiss that she leaned into, grasping my upper arms.

I ended the kiss as a thought entered my mind. "Where is *Carlos* staying tonight?"

"With me."

"So am I, then."

Reaching up to lay a soft hand on my cheek, she said, "Okay."

"There you are. Your stepmom is looking for you, El," this Carlos motherfucker said, creeping up on us.

El?

"Oh, okay. Carlos, you remember Armand? Armand, this is my friend Carlos."

To keep from putting my foot in Carlos's ass, I said, "I'll see you at your place later," and headed back inside the house.

ELLA

"Are you going to tell me what the hell that was?" Carlos inquired as he drove us back to my place. The party was still going strong when I decided to leave before Armand literally exploded.

"What are you talking about?" I asked as I read Armand's response to my *heading home* text.

Armand: *I'm headed your way.*

"Okay, so you wanna play games tonight? Let me be real specific with you then, BFF. Why did I catch you outside your uncle's house with Armand Daniels' tongue down your throat, and why did he look like he was a millisecond from pouncing on me every time I had the displeasure of looking at him?"

"He's spending the night at my place tonight," was how I chose to answer him.

"I knew it! I knew it! You are fucking his crazy ass, aren't you?"

"He's not crazy."

"Ella Juanita McClain! Are you in love?!"

"No, of course not. I...like him. A lot."

"Wait, wait...you're doing your BDSM thing with him? He's *letting* you do it?!"

"I don't kiss and tell, and you know it."

"Well, whatever is going on is about to drive him to murder. I'ma stay locked up in my little guest room tonight."

"Yeah, you probably should," I mumbled.

"What?"

"Nothing."

NINETEEN

ELLA

When I opened the door for him, I could virtually feel him still vibrating. Any other woman probably would've been afraid of him, and maybe I should've been afraid of him, too, but I wasn't. Truth was, angry Armand was just as attractive as submissive Armand.

He looked at me, then over my shoulder. "Where is he?"

"Why, so you can beat him up?" I asked. "Come in, Armand, and talk to me."

With his hands in the pockets of his slacks, he entered my home. As I closed the door and armed the alarm, he repeated, "Where is he, Ella?"

I reached for his hand, waited until he took mine, and led him to my living room.

ARMAND

This nigga was sitting on the sofa like he was waiting on me or something. He was big, tall too. But I was taller and crazy as fuck. I was good at fighting, and right then, I was mad enough to disappear his ass. The second I saw Him standing in my mom's living room with his arm around my damn sir, I knew he'd fucked her. It might not have been recent, but he had definitely fucked her. I was willing to put money on that. Was he gay? Didn't matter. Gay or not, he needed to keep his fucking hands off her.

"Hey, man...I think there's been a misunderstanding. I'm not sure what y'all got going on because Ella is so damn private nowadays, but we're friends. I love her like a sister," dude said in this deep-ass voice.

Fuck him *and* his voice!

"A sister you fucked? Because I know y'all fucked. That shit is written all over you," I spat.

"Armand—" Ella began, but dude interrupted her.

"We did like five years ago, and I didn't like it. As a matter of fact, I hated it. Now you've obviously fucked her, so you should know that's a problem. I'm gay. I was fighting it. After being with her, I realized I couldn't fight it anymore. She was the first person I told, or rather, *she* told *me*. I was a football player, and she kept my secret because it would've been dangerous for people to find out."

"I did, and we became good friends who love and respect each other too much to ever go there again," Ella added.

"Look, I'ma leave you two to talk or whatever. Good night," dude said, leaving the living room.

"Where he sleeping?" I asked.

"Not with us. Come on. Let's go to bed," she coaxed, and of course I followed her.

WE SHOWERED SEPARATELY, although she offered for us to do it together. I knew she was trying to calm me down. She was probably afraid I'd kick dude's door in and kill him if she left me unsupervised, but I was good, better than usual. I hadn't blacked out, at least not yet. Honestly, I wanted her so bad that my anger started dissipating the second she shut and locked the bedroom door behind us. So by the time I'd showered and climbed into bed, I was more than horny.

She pressed her body against mine as soon as my ass hit the sheets, both of us naked, my dick hard enough to lift weights on its own.

Softly, she said, "Did you really believe I'd break our agreement and see someone else? For this to work, you have to trust me...totally."

Wrapping an arm around her, I replied, "I do trust *you*. I don't trust *him* or much of anybody else."

"So you think I can't handle him? Really?"

"Point taken. Can I ask you something?"

"Of course."

"You ain't mad about me not calling you sir all night, for looking you in the eye, for talking without permission?"

"No."

"Why?"

"Because what we do is for us, not for public consumption. Consent is a huge part of BDSM. I don't believe in doing public kink because it can be triggering for some people."

"Plus, you don't want people in your business."

"Bingo."

"How'd you get into this? Into kink?"

She was silent for so long I almost wished I hadn't asked, but I wanted to know. Finally, she answered with, "Believe it or not, it was part of my treatment."

"Treatment? For what?"

I felt her move, and then a lamp popped on beside the bed. She sat up and sighed, her eyes locked on my face. "I...I was very depressed for a while after uh, you know what happened with my last relationship. Depressed, suicidal, and I started taking pills, so I went to a rehab center in LA. They held some rather interesting views on BDSM and how it can help you cope, stuff like that. It actually did help me, and I grew to love the lifestyle."

"How I ain't know you went to rehab?"

"Because money can buy a lot of things, including discretion and strict confidentiality."

"Right. So...am I your first sub?"

"No, I've had a couple others, one I never even met in person. We had an online relationship. You are my first sexual sub, though."

"Word?"

She nodded. "Word."

I chuckled. "Hey, why you let me fuck you instead of you fucking me the other day after you beat my ass?"

"I beat your thighs."

"Same thing."

Smiling, she informed me, "Because you needed to. Just like you need to right now. You need to, you want to, and I want you to."

I stared at her for a minute before grabbing her arm and pulling her down to me, kissing her like my life depended on it. Flipping us, I settled between her thighs, my dick pinned against her pussy, and let my mouth slide to her neck and then her breasts, sucking hard on each nipple as she moaned my name. I wanted to ease inside her, but I couldn't. I needed to be surrounded by her, to feel all of her heat and wetness, to experience the fullness of her tightness all at once, so I slammed into her, closing my eyes and smiling when she breathlessly groaned, "You're such a fucking savage and I love it! Fuck me, Armand, and don't stop."

So I eased back and slammed into her again. "This pussy... shit!" I mumbled. "So good..."

"Ohhhh, Armand! Armand!"

"Ella...sir...thank you for this pussy. Thank you for this good-ass pussy! I wanna know everything about you. I want inside your head, baby. I love this. I love being with you," I whimpered.

That was how it went—me pile driving into her pussy, alternating sucking her tongue and her titties while I strummed her clit and said all kinds of shit—all true.

She got hers first, her body jerking and seizing for so long that I was almost afraid the orgasm had triggered some kind of seizure. Then it was my turn. I can say I held out longer than my usual, and she didn't lie. The release had me floating outside my body.

Afterwards, I left the bed for the bathroom. When I returned with a warm, wet washcloth and began cleaning her up, she lazily asked, "Is this that aftercare shit?"

Grinning, I said, "Yes, sir...it is."

ELLA

Carlos cooked breakfast for us the next morning, and I had to basically drag Armand out of bed to the kitchen to eat with us. He wore his slacks and a white wife beater. Even with the dredges of sleep clinging to him, he was absolutely gorgeous. It was obvious that Carlos was taking note of that, too.

Staring down at the food before him, Armand said, "This looks good. You ain't poison it or nothing, did you?"

Carlos laughed. "Naw, man. Eat up. I hope you like Denver omelets."

"I do," Armand said, still staring at the plate.

Rolling my eyes, I asked. "You wanna switch with me?"

"Nah, I don't want you to die, either. I couldn't take that shit," Armand said, finally taking a bite. He nodded, and I grinned over at Carlos.

No sexy NBA players were poisoned in my home that day.

YOU THINK *you're better than On One because you came from money. You ain't shit!*

I still can't believe you did On One like that, missed his memorial to go to a basketball game! You just wanted to be seen.

Bitch.

I used to think she was nice. Now I hate her.

Somebody needs to kick her ass!

FUCK YOU ELLA MCCLAIN!

She's canceled!

"Why haven't you been using security since you've been in St. Louis?" my dad asked, pulling me from reading the comments on my latest post—a picture of that morning's sunrise—back into our conversation.

I fought not to sigh into the phone. "Because I don't need it here. I'm practically a hermit. I don't really go anywhere except to Uncle Leland's house and the Cyclones home games. I have my groceries delivered or do *QuickEats*. My property is gated, and I have an alarm system."

"Ella—"

"Daddy, *please*. I just want some normalcy. That's one of the reasons I moved here, remember?"

He *did* sigh into the phone. "Princess, these people on social media have lost their damn minds. Do you not see the comments they're leaving you, threatening you because you didn't go to One's memorial? You've got to take your safety seriously."

"I *am*. If I decide to venture out more, I'll use security. I used it when I traveled to Paris, didn't I?"

"Yeah, how was Paris? I've been meaning to ask you about that."

"Mom showed up."

"Well, you know how she and Claude can be. They share a strange friendship. They either love each other or hate each other to extremes."

"Yeah. So anyway, I left early because of it. I'm good, though."

"Good. Ella, is there something going on with you and Armand Daniels? I saw him staring at you during the party. I know that look."

"Daddy..."

"Is it that he just wants you? Because I know you're not entertaining the thought of—"

"Daddy!"

"All right, all right. You're grown but understand this...I will *kill* his ass. You got me? Leland doesn't think he'd be that stupid but that's 'cause he's married to his mama. I don't put anything past niggas, especially *that* little nigga."

"Oh my god," I groaned.

"God is the only somebody who'll be able to save his ass; that's a promise."

TWENTY

ARMAND

Tired wasn't the word. I was literally on my last leg after fucking Ella like a caveman half the night and getting my ass kicked at practice this afternoon. Then there were the meetings, phone calls, and my weekly therapy session with Mr. Charles. I couldn't wait to get a nap in. I didn't even bother going to my bedroom when I made it home, collapsing right on the sofa, legs hanging over the arm. I was just dozing off when a knock sounded at the front door. I couldn't remember if I locked it but muttered, "Come in!" without realizing what I was saying.

My eyes were closed, and I was almost asleep again when I heard, "Boogie? Did I wake you?"

My eyes popped open to see my mother standing over me. "Ma? I...what's up?"

"If you're asleep, it can wait. I know how tired y'all are after practice," she offered.

I rubbed my eyes and sat up when the text message alert

dinged on my phone. "Nah, you good. What? You kicking me out?" I quipped.

Taking a seat next to me, she smiled and shook her head. "No. Having you here so close to me is a dream come true, especially since you seem so much...calmer?"

As I read Ella's "Hey" message, I asked, "You think so?"

"I do," my mom said. "Boogie...can I ask you something?"

Setting my phone on my thigh, I gave her my full attention. "Yeah, what's up?"

"Are...are you and Ella seeing each other?"

"Uh..."

"I'm only asking because I sensed an attraction between y'all. I noticed it that first night we all had dinner together. You like her and she definitely likes you."

I frowned. "You really think she likes me?"

"I *know* she does, and I suspect you know it, too."

I shrugged and bit back a smile as I dropped my gaze to the coffee table, concentrating on the big candle sitting on it.

"I think it's nice. I think...I like the idea of the two of you together," my mom shared.

I snapped my head up. "You do?"

She smiled. "I do. I know you, Boogie. I know your heart, and I see you're trying to get better. I believe in you. Always have."

Damn, now she had me about to cry, and as private as I knew Ella was, I still said, "I don't wanna hurt her. *Ever*. I...I never meant to hurt you. I never did, Mama," my voice shaking.

She pulled me into her arms, and I said fuck it and let the tears flow. "I know. I know," she cooed, "and if you don't want to hurt her, you won't. You love her?"

"I don't know. I just know I like being around her. I..."

"Yeah. Hey, look at me."

I backed out of her arms and lifted my eyes to her face. "Ma'am?"

"I haven't told Leland. It's not my business to."

I nodded.

She kissed my cheek and stood from the sofa. "I'll let you get your rest. If you need to talk about anything, I'm *always* here for you."

"Thank you, Ma."

After she left, I picked up my phone and replied to Ella with: *Hey, sir.*

Her response came almost instantly: *You done with practice?*

Me: *Yes, sir.*

Her: *Good. Pack a bag and come here.*

I was still tired as shit, but I quickly replied with: *On my way, sir.*

ELLA

His eyes were on the open case I'd placed on the floor—my toolkit. It was a black case with plush pink interior and compartments that held the tools of the Fem-dom trade: a flogger, paddle, riding crop, ball gag, nipple clamps, cock rings, rope, tape, candles, and blindfolds. I'd removed the butt plugs since I knew they might set him off. He was waiting for me to choose which of the toys we'd play with. I already knew; I just liked seeing him like this—on his knees, head bowed, hands behind his back, power jumping off him like electrical sparks from a live wire.

Finally, I moved the case from the floor to the bed and said, "Lie on your stomach, arms down beside your body, head to the side."

Without uttering a word, he spread his naked body over the pink rug on my bedroom floor as I lit the candle, waiting for the wax near the flame to begin to melt. Once it did, I warned, "This will sting."

He nodded.

Moving to stand with one foot on either side of his body, I held the candle so that the wax dripped onto the beautiful brown skin of his back and smiled when he flinched and grunted softly. Drip after drip landed on his back, and I could feel myself getting wetter and wetter as he took the pain with little movement. His grunts became moans, so I asked him, "You like that, Armand? You like feeling that sting?"

"Yes, sir," he rumbled.

"Hmm, turn over," I ordered. "On your back, arms at your sides, eyes on me."

I watched him flip over, his eyelids heavy as he licked his lips.

"Keep your eyes on me, Armand. Pay close attention."

"Yes, sir," he groaned as I widened my stance over him and used my fingers to part my labia. I was naked, too, of course. I found my button and began massaging it while one hand cupped my right breast. I stroked and stroked myself, dipped a finger inside me, and then brought it to my mouth to taste. "Mmmm," I hummed. "I do taste good."

His Adam's apple bobbed up and down as he stared at me, dick standing at attention. With a smile, I went back to work pleasuring myself, massaging my clit, sliding two fingers into my pussy this time, and as I brought my fingers to my mouth again, I asked, "Do you want to taste me, Armand?"

He nodded vigorously. "Yes, sir. *Please.*"

I lowered myself to sit right on his dick, placing my fingers in his mouth and smiling as he eagerly lapped at them. Lifting my body, I squatted over him, taking his dick, and sliding it between my wet folds. Closing my eyes, I rubbed him over my clit faster and faster, my moans loud in my ears as the compounding pressure in my core erupted, my body shuddering over his until I collapsed onto him.

"Sir...sir, I need...can I fuck you, or you fuck me? It don't matter. I gotta feel your pussy, sir," he pleaded.

I nodded against his chest before lifting again, taking him in my hand and guiding him inside me. “You can use your hands,” I mumbled, and he quickly gripped my ass cheeks as I rode him and rode him and rode him...

TWENTY-ONE

ARMAND

This was my favorite thing —after care. We'd been deep in this thing, this arrangement, for like three months now, so deep that I couldn't remember the last time I slept at the cottage on my mom's property. If I wasn't on the road with the Cyclones, I was at Ella's place, and as much as I loved everything else she did to me, it was the way she took care of me that had my heart and soul wide open.

This time, after bathing me, she wrapped me up in this furry comforter thing and we sat on the sofa together watching a nature show about the coral reef while she fed me some peanut butter cookies she made. They were good as hell, too.

"Either I baked the shit out of these cookies, or they really are your favorite," Ella said, handing me my bottled water for the tenth time. "Drink some more, baby."

I took a swig and nodded. "Both, sir."

She kissed my cheek, and I turned my head to kiss her lips. Then we sat there and stared at each other until she looked away.

We had a connection, a *real* connection that neither of us could deny, but she was fighting it. I guess I understood why, though. For all my therapy and the way BDSM was helping me deal with my stuff, I was still *me*. If I were her, I'd fight that shit, too. However, I couldn't fight what I was feeling for her, and I didn't want to. She made me feel like I was the most important thing in the world to her. Even when she used me for her pleasure, it was still all about me. It took me a minute to realize it, even though I'd run across this truth during my required reading, but I now knew I held the power in our dynamic. I could give consent or revoke it. Ella couldn't Dominate me unless I submitted to her. She needed me as much as I needed her.

"Sir," I began, "can I ask you something?"

"You know you can," she replied, her eyes on the TV.

"I got one good friend in this world, one guy I trust with my life. For a long time, I considered him the brother I never had, and...he's engaged now. I don't really know his girl. I've only been around her a couple times. I...they invited me over to dinner...and I want you to go with me."

I watched her, observed the unchanged expression on her face. Ella was an expert at appearing to be blank when I knew that was never the case with her.

"I know how you are about privacy," I continued, "but this is my boy. If I ask him to keep things confidential, he will. I wouldn't put you out there like that. I know how crazy motherfuckers can get, and I would kick the whole world's ass before I let someone hurt you—physically or emotionally. I—"

"Okay," she softly said.

"What?" I asked, thinking I was for sure hearing things.

Finally facing me, something foreign in her eyes, she repeated, "Okay. I'll go."

"Thank you, sir."

Smiling, she leaned in to kiss me. "You're welcome, baby."

We were in bed later that night and she was fast asleep when I realized what I'd seen in her eyes and why it seemed so foreign to me. It was fear, but what exactly was she afraid of?

ELLA

"I've been...I'm involved with Armand Daniels," I blurted into the phone.

In response, Carlos asserted, "Okay...also, grass is green, there's fish in the ocean, I like dick, two plus two is four, beardless Drake looks like an unfortunate Latino uncle, sugar DOES NOT go on grits—"

"Okay, okay! I get it! I'm stating the obvious!"

"The *painfully* obvious. I heard you screaming like a white chick in a horror movie the night of his mom's party. I was like, is he fucking her or killing her, but I wasn't about to do a wellness check and get my ass beat to death. That's some good dick, huh?"

"What the hell kind of best friend are you, Carlos?! I'm trying to share a part of me with you that I previously kept private!"

"You avoided the question, so it must be excellent!"

"Carlos!"

"All right, so...you're opening up about him. That must mean you've caught feelings, and if you have, I am not going to judge you...because damn! If you won't tell me about the dick, at least tell me this, is dude as fine naked as he is with clothes on?"

"He's a damn work of art. Lean, muscular, always smells good. Even his sweat smells good. He's...I shouldn't be doing this. Not with him."

"Then why are you?"

I sighed. "Full disclosure? I was and am attracted to him. I like..."

"Danger? Insanity? Living on the edge?"

"Apparently so. First Jackson, now Armand. Only difference is everyone thinks Jackson was this noble guy."

"And you're letting them continue to believe that because..."

"Because he's dead. What good would it do to tarnish his legacy?"

"Well, for one, it would stop his rabid-ass fans from cyber bullying you because you missed his memorial months ago. He's been gone for two years! Damn!"

"I know. I had to block his sister. She kept texting me saying I'm breaking their mom's heart. His mom hasn't contacted me since I missed the memorial. I guess I could've at least told her I wasn't coming on the phone rather than texting her..."

"His mom knows the truth. He gaslit her, too. Jackson "On One" Reynolds was a very talented and handsome, drug-abusing narcissist who knew how to play a role for the public. How many times would he hug and kiss on you for the cameras then berate you or worse for not smiling enough or some other bullshit in private..."

As Carlos continued to speak, I let my mind drift back to all the times Jackson made me feel like I wasn't enough, like I was inferior and lucky to be with him. Things didn't start out that way because people like him, narcissists, are experts at doing what needs to be done to reel you in. The love-bombing feels like heaven, but they are just as good at gaslighting and being outright cruel. Loving Jackson broke me. Trying to save him nearly destroyed me, and now? Now I had Armand who I cared about and who I believed truly cared about me, but I was scared. Scared of more cyber bullying. Scared of being hurt again, or worse, hurting him.

"...I hate to bring all this shit up, but fuck them folks! Them folks being the fans, Jackson's family, and even your family if need be. I know they love you, but everyone sees you as a little girl. They ain't gotta know you like to beat dude's asses, but eventually, everyone is going to have to understand you're a grown woman. If being involved with crazy-ass Armand Daniels is a mistake, it's *yours* to make. Period!" Carlos finished.

Smiling I said, "And that's on Mary had a little lamb."

TWENTY-TWO

ARMAND

"What did you tell your friend about us?" she asked. I could feel her pretty, dark eyes on me as I drove us to Scotty's place.

"Whatchu mean, sir?" I replied, glancing over at her. She looked too damn good in ripped jeans and a blue and white collared shirt. I'd sat and watched her get her makeup and hair done, although she didn't need it. Ella was a damn diva, but I liked that about her, just like I liked everything else about her.

"I mean, you told them you were bringing me, right?"

"I told them I was bringing a friend who's very private. I ain't say it was you."

"Oh, a friend..."

"What you wanted me to say, that I was bringing my Dom? That's between us, right?"

"You would admit I'm your Dom to your friend?"

"Scotty? Yeah. Other niggas? Probably not. I ain't close enough to nobody else to share shit with."

"Hmmm."

"Hmm, what!"

"Nothing. I...nothing."

"You nervous, sir?"

"No..." she said unconvincingly.

"You are THE Ella McClain. You ain't got shit to be nervous about. You the baddest motherfucker around. I'm a legend for having you on my arm."

She reached over and squeezed my thigh. "Keep this up and you might get edged tonight."

"Word? I tell you how you got the dopest toes I've ever seen?"

She laughed and so did I.

"Um...your friends aren't On One fans, are they?"

"It don't matter. They say one fucked-up thing to you and I'ma go to jail tonight. On god, I am."

"O...kay," she said, dragging the word out.

Once we made it to Scotty's building, I hopped out of my Cullinan and opened the door for her, offering her my hand. In her red, high heel shoes, she was as tall as me.

I liked that shit, too, so much so that I grabbed the side of her neck and pulled her into a kiss.

"You are such a damn savage," she moaned once the kiss ended.

So I kissed her again, biting her tongue this time. "You can punish me for that later, sir."

"Oh, I will," she promised as I led her toward the building.

"CAN you please close your mouth, nigga?" I said to Scotty. Dude had opened the door, and once he saw Ella, his mouth fell open and hadn't closed since. "And can we come inside?"

Mouth still open, he nodded and backed out of the doorway.

Ella gave me a concerned look and squeezed my hand as we stepped inside.

"He gon' be all right. Just being goofy as fuck right now," I said, giving her a smile that she didn't return.

"Bae, was that the door—ohhhhh, shit! That's Ella McClain and she's so beautiful!" Rory gushed, rushing toward Ella, who in turn, stepped closer to me. Rory seemed oblivious to the fact that she was freaking Ella out, though. "I love your dad's music! And I loved that spread you did for the December issue of *Elle*. Damn, you're tall!"

Ella gave her a tiny smile. "Yeah...runs in the family."

"Wait, y'all related, ain't you? So that's why you brought her?" Scotty asked, finally breaking out of his trance.

"By marriage, and no, that ain't why I brought her," I stated.

Scotty frowned before his eyes widened and he said, "Ohhhhh, okay. I gotcha. Wooooow. Like, for real, wooooow." Then he glanced at his girl. "Rory, this is Armand. Y'all met before, remember?"

"Yes!" Rory chirped.

"'Sup, Rory," I greeted the small woman. "Scotty, Rory—"

"Aurora," Rory corrected me. Shit, I didn't even know Rory wasn't her real name.

Looking at my old friend, I asked, "You Scotty or Burgess?"

He gave me a smirk.

I held my free hand up, the other still fastened to Ella's. "Just asking. Anyway...this is Ella McClain, as y'all already know."

"Hi," Ella said softly, squeezing my hand again.

"YOU COOKED THIS, SCOTTY?" I asked after swallowing another heap of food.

"Yeah, I be cheffing my ass off up in here," Scotty proudly confirmed.

"Oh, word? So, you a regular Gordon Ramsey up in this bitch! Gon' open you a restaurant?"

He shrugged.

"The food's delicious. Best salmon I've ever had," Ella said from her seat beside me.

I nudged her. "You ain't gotta lie, sir—Ella. You done had all kinds of gourmet shit, plus you can burn yourself."

"Oh, really? You been cooking for this fool?" Scotty asked.

"You cook at all?" Rory trilled.

With a smile, Ella divulged, "I like to cook. Armand reaps the benefit of that quite often." Her hand met my thigh and I swear my dick shot to attention.

"Okaaaaay!" Scotty's silly ass said in this high-pitched voice. "I see you, Daniels!"

"Um, can I use your bathroom?" Ella asked, prompting poor Rory to hop up from her seat so fast, she damn near knocked the dinner table over.

"Sure! Let me show you where it is!" Rory offered.

Lifting from her seat, Ella rested a hand on my shoulder. "Be right back."

Licking my lips, I nodded, and she just stood there staring at me for a moment before bending over and kissing me dead in the mouth. Shit, I almost came right then and there.

I was watching Ella and Rory leave the room when I heard Scotty hiss, "Are you out yo' fuckin' mind?!"

Swinging my head around to face him, I said, "What?"

"You're fucking Ella McClain? Your stepdaddy's niece? Big South's daughter? On One's girl?"

"No, I'm fucking Ella McClain, a *grown ass woman.* Her name stands alone. All those other folks don't define her. Believe me, she's her own woman."

He raised his hands. "Damn, okay."

"And I don't wanna hear shit about it. I don't care what nobody thinks. I ain't stopping what we got." He stared at me, and I barked, "What?!"

He shrugged. "Nothing, just thinking about what I'ma buy with that hunnid you owe me, because she got your ass on lock. Nigga, you're in love."

"I..." I closed my mouth because I couldn't protest or agree. I honestly didn't know what I felt for her. I just knew I needed her, wanted her, and would legit off a nigga over her. If that meant I loved her then so be it.

Once she returned to the table, she gave me a smile and another kiss, and I'd be damned if that kiss didn't feel like she loved me, too.

TWENTY-THREE

ELLA

This was my first time going to one of Armand's games in a while, mostly because of our...situation. When he knew I was in the crowd, his eyes constantly found me. I wasn't sure if he was even conscious of it half the time, but I did know he didn't need the distraction. I'd opted to attend this home game because Kim had invited me, saying she missed us hanging out together. I couldn't tell her I was spending all my time with her son who'd all but moved in with me at that point.

As we watched the shoot-around, Kim leaned in and whispered, "How are things going with you two?"

I turned to look at her, saw the knowing in her eyes, and frowned. "He...Armand told you?"

"He didn't have to," she said. "And I haven't told a soul. I'm just...I'm happy he has you."

Looking up in time to see him grinning at me, I said, "I'm happy to have him, too."

. . .

"YOU MISSED IT. I'm not surprised, though. Everything else is more important to you than me."

I held the phone to my ear as I followed my bodyguard, Hernandez, through the relatively small but congested Santorini airport to my gate. "Jackson, I had a shoot. I've been working. I'm heading back to the states now. You knew I wasn't going to be there."

"You could've missed that shit. You ain't a real model. They just hiring you because of who your folks are. You don't need that. You shoulda been here with me! I was nervous as shit before I went onstage."

Sighing, I saw that we'd made it to the gate, so I fell into a seat. "You've done tons of festivals before, including that one. You did a bunch before we ever met. You didn't need me there back then, and this is what I love doing."

"More than you love me? Everybody was asking about you. I looked like a simp telling them you were too busy to be here. Man, stop playing with that modeling shit!"

"I will when you stop playing with your rapping shit," I tossed back at him.

"That's real fucked up. You know that ain't the same thing. I'm a platinum-selling artist. I got Grammys. What you got? A couple perfume ads in *People* magazine?"

"Fuck you," I hissed.

"See, this bullshit is why I gotta take pills. Your childish ass is always stressing me out..."

"Ella, they're ready for you."

I snapped out of my reverie and smiled at the assistant standing next to me. Pulling myself together, I stepped from the shade of the tent out onto the sands of Gialos Beach in a red Versace swimsuit, a white cover-up flowing in the breeze behind me.

TWENTY-FOUR

ARMAND

"This has been an interesting season for you, Armand, and now the Cyclones are out of the playoffs. Detroit is a favorite to win the conference championship. Do you feel the trade ruined your chances at a ring?" this nerdy looking dude asked. I wasn't even sure what network or website he was from. Honestly, I was out of practice when it came to this stuff. I couldn't even remember how many times I got in trouble with teams for refusing to do press. It really was a miracle I was still in the league.

Hands on my hips and sweat pasting my jersey to my back, I shook my head. "Nah, I'm good with the trade. The Cyclones is a solid team full of some of the best players in the league. This just wasn't our year."

Dude looked shocked as fuck, so I smiled and added, "We did our best, all of us, and next season, we'll do even better."

"Uh...thanks, Armand."

With a smile on my face, I nodded. "No problem, man."

. . .

I WAS in the locker room, the results of a tough game settling into my joints and muscles as I pulled my jersey over my head, trying to decide if I was going to shower here or at home. Ella was in Greece, so I didn't see the point in doing it here. I missed her, and she'd only been gone a couple days.

I closed my eyes for a few seconds, trying to summon the energy to even stand up. I'd planned to skip the cryo room, but I was rethinking that decision.

"Damn, what happened to your back, Daniels?" I opened my eyes and turned to see Drayveon Walker grinning at me as he added, "You been tearing that thang up, huh? Back all red and shit."

Other teammates joined in, including McClain, which felt awkward, but dude was funny. I could admit that.

"Damn, what she do to you? It don't look like regular fingernails. You messing around with a werewolf?" Leland quipped. These niggas were literally gathered around me staring at my back. It was candle wax, but I wasn't about to tell them that. Ella had dropped that shit all over my back, sucked my dick until I was delirious, and rode me to nirvana the night before she left for Greece.

Damn, I really, *really* missed her.

Grinning, I said, "Man, fuck y'all," as I stood and headed to the cryo room with these dudes still roasting me as I left.

ELLA

Me: *What are you doing?*

Him: *Not shit, sir. Missing you. Be glad when you come home.*

I smiled.

Me: *You at my place or yours?*

Him: Mine, sir.

Me: *Why? You have a key to mine. You can use it. You forgot the gate and alarm codes?*

Him: *No. just wouldn't feel right to be there without you, sir.*

Me: *Sorry you guys lost but I'm proud of how you handled that interview. Super proud.*

Him: *Thanks. You saw that?*

Him: *I mean, you saw that, sir?*

I was smiling so hard my cheeks hurt.

Me: *I did. I watched it online. Hey, I miss you, too.*

Him: *You do, sir?*

Me: *Yes. Very much.*

I waited a few seconds before adding: *So the season is over for you now?*

Him: *Yes, sir. I'm kinda glad about it. I'm tired as shit, sir.*

Me: *I know you are. Have you ever been to the Maldives?*

Him: *Huh? Nah, I can't even spell that shit.*

Now, I was laughing.

Me: *You just read it in my text!*

Him: *Oh right.*

Me: *Meet me in the Maldives, Armand.*

Him: *When, sir?*

TWENTY-FIVE

ARMAND

We were on the patio of our overwater bungalow. Well, I was lying on my back on the patio, ropes binding my arms to the sides of my body. Ella was on my face, riding the hell out of my tongue, moaning, and whimpering my name while I worked the strongest muscle in my body. The sun was high in the sky, the water was still, and we were both full of seafood and bourbon and wine. This woman, *my sir*, was everything to me, and at that very moment, I knew I would slay a million dragons for her.

She grabbed my locs, clutching them tightly as she stilled on my face, a long grunt rising from her belly and shooting out of her mouth. I kept licking, dipping my tongue inside her and lapping up all she had to offer. When she finally came down from her high, she slid from my face, moved over my chest, and landed square on my dick, grinding on it as she gripped my neck with her soft hand and kissed my wet face before sucking my tongue. As her grip on my neck tightened, she used her other hand to guide me inside her, making me croak, "Ohhhhh, sir! Ah! Damn!"

Her hand slid from my neck to my nipple, squeezing it as she rode me, and I hissed, "Fuck, sir! Shit!"

When she hopped up off me, I missed her pussy so much that I wanted to cry. Instead, I caught a glimpse of a view that rivaled the one surrounding us, her naked ass as she stepped inside the bungalow, quickly returning with a pink vibrator in hand.

"Damn, you brought your whole kit here, sir?"

"No, I had the butler purchase some things for me," she answered.

"So, the butler knows what we over here doing...sir?"

"Anybody within a mile of us with half a sense of hearing knows what we've been doing, as loud as we both are."

I smiled. "Facts. So...uhhhhh, what you gonna do with that vibrator, sir?"

She rolled her eyes. "It ain't for you or your ass region, Armand. It's for me."

"Oh..." I still wasn't sure what she was going to do with it, and when she squatted over me and slid back down on my dick, I stopped caring altogether. My eyes were closed and I was floating when I heard the buzzing of the vibrator, followed by a jerking movement from her. When I lifted my head, pressing my chin into my chest, I saw the most beautiful sight. She was bouncing up and down on my erection while holding the pink vibrator against her clit with her head thrown back. I watched her and felt her and felt her and watched her, witnessing the exact moment she hit her peak, her ride becoming sloppy and uncoordinated, her grip on the vibrator loosening until it was bumping against my dick while her walls shuddered around me, and the shit felt...good. So good, that I loudly moaned, "Oh, fuck!"

Then the vibrator was gone, and she was on her knees still riding me while squeezing both my nipples—*hard*.

"Sir...sir...sir...I...shit!!!!!!"

And that was it.

Game. Over.

"SIR, where you learn all this shit, like the vibrator thing? In therapy?" I asked.

"No. I'm just...experienced," she answered.

"Me, too. Been with a lot of women, but no one like you."

"There's definitely only one me."

We were in the bed, naked and fresh out the shower, and she was massaging my arms. "I have something I want to give you," she told me.

"You do, sir? What?"

She kissed me before lifting from the bed and digging in one of her ten or so suitcases. Her back was to me when she said, "Close your eyes and sit up on the side of the bed."

I did, waiting impatiently for whatever she was going to give me. I high-key hoped it was some more pussy. I couldn't get enough of that.

I felt her climb into the bed with me, felt her soft lips meet my back and almost whimpered. She placed something cold around my neck and said, "Go look in the mirror."

I stood, walking into the bathroom and observing myself in the huge mirror that hung over the double sink vanity. Behind me, I could see her approaching, and as she wrapped her arms around me, I reached up and touched the diamond Cuban link chain. It was fat as hell, heavy, and short, almost like a choker.

"I like it, sir. But why? You ain't have to give me nothing. You already give me more than enough."

She rested her head on my back and said, "You make me happy and I wanna keep you forever."

"You got me forever, then. You make me happy, too."

"I'm...this chain is my way of collaring you. It's discreet, so no one else has to know what it means." Her voice was soft, shaky.

I tried to turn to face her, but she squeezed her arms around me. "No. I want us to stay like this," she said.

"Okay...collar me...I read about that. When a Dom collars a sub, it means they own them, right?" I queried.

"Yes."

"So, if I accept this, I'm accepting that you own me, sir?"

"Y-yes."

"Then you don't need this chain. Sir, you owned me from the first moment you touched me."

"Armand...turn around," she whispered.

I did, my heart aching at the sight of tears flooding her pretty face. "Ella, sir...what's wrong?"

Swiping at her nose, she whimpered, "I wanna get this right. I don't want to hurt you or make you want to hurt yourself."

"Why would you ever think you could hurt me?"

"Because..."

TWENTY-SIX

ELLA

Two years earlier...

Things with Jackson started out sweet, slow, and beautiful. He was signed to my father's record label when he was like twenty. I was still in high school at the time and didn't meet him or really get to know him as a friend until I moved in with my dad during my junior year. We kept in touch casually, mostly through social media. He had a lot of girlfriends before me, and I had a bit of a crush on him from the day I met him.

One weekend during my second year of college in Texas, he DM'd me on IG letting me know he was in town and wanted to kick it with me. We had dinner, talked, really clicked. A month or so later, we became officially exclusive and public. My dad knew and liked him, so that was a plus because he is ridiculously over-protective.

We were good for about six months. He'd come visit me or fly me out to wherever he was to visit him on weekends, and somehow, I managed to keep my grades up. He was always sending me gifts. He was sweet to me.

I spent a lot of time with him during my spring and summer breaks. My third year of college, I started pursuing modeling. I didn't get a lot of gigs, but I did pretty good for a newbie. Initially, Jackson supported my modeling journey, but as it demanded more and more of my time, he began to complain.

Then there were the pills, which I knew about from the beginning but rarely saw him take them. As the months turned into years and his fame increased, the pills became more prevalent. The more pills, the meaner and more demanding of my time he became. He tried to talk me into getting pregnant more than once, but I wasn't *that* gullible. He would accuse me of saying things I never said, of hiding his pills, of telling him he wasn't as good as my father. It got to the point where I started believing I was actually doing and saying the stuff he accused me of, that I deserved to be yelled at and...hurt.

I was young, *so young*, but I loved him. He killed that love, though, with every demand he made of me, every belittling word he said to me, every gaslighting episode, and every time he put his hands on me. The times he got physical were few, but they were enough. I tried to get along with him. That didn't work. I tried to leave him. That didn't work. He overdosed once but recovered. He blamed that overdose on me leaving him.

The night he died, I was so preoccupied; I was barely listening to him as he ranted. He was full of pills, which made him groggy and slow. He was slurring his words, rambling about me not being there when he needed me because I'd been traveling for work.

I'd turned to say something to him, to tell him it was over, like *for real* over, but stopped when I saw him downing more pills. I was just so used to it. It never occurred to me that maybe he was going to overdose again. Hell, he could easily take twenty pills before noon.

I left him on the couch. I just left him there and went to bed. When I woke up the next morning, he was dead. He'd been dead for a while. The coroner said he more than likely died less than an hour after he took those pills. Percocet, Oxy, whatever. He walked around with a pharmacy in his pockets every day. Those pills killed him, and I slept all night with his dead body in that condo with me.

I think...I think a part of me wanted him to die. I think I was glad he did.

ELLA

Now...

"You said he put his hands on you? He...he *hit* you?" Armand's voice was so tight; it made me flinch.

"Yes," I confirmed.

We were back in the bed in our beautiful villa, surrounded by blue ocean as we both fell silent. I watched as he visibly tried to quell his anger.

"He's gone, Armand. He's...he's dead," I said.

"I know, just pissed that *I* didn't kill him," he gritted.

"Armand..."

"Does anyone else know what he did to you, how he treated you?"

"I'm...his mom saw him hit me a couple times. His sister, too, and I told my stepmom and my therapist. He never lashed out at me or hit me in public or in front of our show's crew. Everybody believed he was a great guy, including my family because he knew how to play that role so well."

"You've kept all of it out of the public, even the drug abuse. Word is he committed suicide because of depression. There have been foundations created in his honor. Hell, I donated to one of them!"

"Yeah, didn't see the point in tarnishing his legacy, and I'm pretty sure he did suffer from depression among other things."

"But his stupid-ass fans are wrecking your reputation. I could fuck every one of them up!"

"Armand, don't—"

"I'm good. I'm good. So, you blame yourself for him dying? Don't. He was fucked up. You didn't put those pills in his hand or his body. You had a right to pursue a career. Fuck him. You didn't hurt him and you've never hurt me."

"I know it's not my fault. Cognitively, *I know that*. I had months of therapy while I was in rehab—"

"Why were you in rehab? For pills, right?"

I nodded as I blinked back tears. "I was so depressed, just messed up. I don't know. I wouldn't leave his condo, and there were freaking pills stashed everywhere. I just wanted the pain to stop, so I started taking them like a dumb ass. I'm too smart for that, but I did it! I ended up in rehab because I lost two whole days one time. I still don't remember what happened during those forty-eight hours, but one day it was Monday, and the next thing I knew, it was Thursday. I asked my dad to help me get into rehab and he did. It saved my life, helped me regain the agency and control Jackson had whittled away, and introduced me to the therapeutic benefits of kink."

He stared at me for long moments before saying, "I don't know much about love other than the kind of love I have for my mom, granny, and my boy Scotty. You know, familial love, but I...I love you, Ella, and I'm yours. Do I need to sign some shit? You own me, sir. You own every part of me...especially my heart."

I burst into tears while pulling him to me, and right before my lips met his, I wept, "I love you, too."

TWENTY-SEVEN

ARMAND

"This is one of my favorite places. I love it here," Ella said through a sigh.

"Yeah, it's beautiful here. Peaceful. Was a time when peace and quiet bothered me," I said as we sat facing each other in the big, circular tub that rested on the patio.

"Why? I'm the opposite. I love serenity."

Shrugging, I lifted her foot from the water, kissing one perfectly painted red toenail. "It's...I guess I grew up with so much chaos, peace just felt strange to me. Alien, really."

"Your mom is so sweet. Was she not a good mother?"

Kissing another toe, I said, "No, she was a wonderful mother. It was her men. All of them, including my father, were assholes who hit her. I would wake up in the middle of the night to her screaming. She had so many black eyes, a broken nose, concussions, and I felt helpless because I was just a kid. You know why I fight so much? I think it's because once I was big enough to fight them, I was able to protect her. I kind of stay in that mode now.

You know, *stay ready so you don't have to get ready*, but...but I have a hard time turning that readiness off when I don't need it."

She leaned forward a little, her breasts appearing to float on the water. "What do you mean?"

"Shit, I ain't said sir in—"

"It's okay. I'll punish you for that later. Just...just talk to me."

I had to smile. "You're a trip, but anyway, I...damn, I think I'm scared to tell you this."

"I told you I slept through Jackson's death. You can tell me anything, or have you stopped trusting me?"

"No...uh, I used to hurt my mom. I never *tried* to, but...now I know I have Intermittent Explosive Disorder. Sometimes, I get so angry that I lose control of myself. Half the time, I barely remember doing the shit. With my mom, it was like, she'd just be in the way. I ain't try to put my hands on her. I'm just fucked up, sir. I'm real fucked up. I love my mom so much. The last time I remember being as happy as I am now is when I was in Miami and she was there with me. She's everything to me. It kills me that I hurt her. I just...I'm defective or something."

"You've never hurt me. Not once, and I've done all kinds of stuff to you."

"I know, but I ain't dumb enough to think I'm cured. I'll probably be fighting this shit for the rest of my life."

"Then I'll fight it with you."

My eyebrows wrinkled up as tears jumped into my eyes. My words came out as a sob. "You care that much about me...sir?"

"Yes, I do," she said, moving to straddle me. Taking my face in her wet hands, she kissed every inch of it, softly saying, "I love you," between each peck. When her mouth finally found mine, I stopped fighting my tears, letting them flow freely as she reached between us and guided me inside her. My mouth fell open and head fell back as she showed me her love until I damn near left my own body.

ELLA

"That ain't the chicken head!" I yelled from my seat on the bed.

"Yeah it is! You just don't know the chicken head when you see it! Look!" Standing at the foot of the bed with the glass patio doors behind him, Armand started doing what I knew to be the cabbage patch.

Laughing, I informed him, "I'm the one with the old parents, so I know what I'm talking about. That ain't the chicken head, Armand DeShawn!"

Grinning, he challenged, "I bet you don't know what this is, though."

Now I was laughing so hard, my stomach started cramping. "Nigga, *that's* the chicken head!"

"Nah, this the running man!"

"OMG, how can you be both black and this confused about dancing?"

His phone began to ring, making him roll his eyes. "That's probably my mom. You lucky she called and saved your ass. I was about to bust out the milly rock."

"I can only imagine which dance you've got that one mixed up with."

I watched as he grabbed his phone from the night table and sat with his back to me. He was naked and so was I. It was hard to think of a time when we weren't nude when we were together, and I wasn't sure if that was because we were just that comfortable with each other or we were just that horny. Maybe both? I wasn't really paying attention to what he was saying, although I'd heard him say his agent's name. I was too busy thinking about how it felt to be with him, how much I loved him, how much he loved me. We were both so shattered, but at the same time, perfect for each other. With his wounds superimposing mine, we were unblemished—healed.

He finally ended the call, turned to me, and said, "That was Nate. He wants to meet with me next week after we get back."

"Oh...where are y'all gonna meet?"

"I'm not sure. Knowing Nate, we'll probably go have lunch somewhere or we'll meet at my place."

"Invite him over to my place for dinner."

He frowned. "For real?"

I nodded. "Yeah."

He sat there and stared at me before saying, "Sir, can I eat your pussy?"

Lifting an eyebrow, I said, "Yes, you may."

And then...well, he ate my pussy.

ARMAND

It was dark, late the night before we were leaving our little piece of paradise to return to the states. The upside was we were taking a private flight. The downside was we were returning to reality. Meetings and stuff for me, modeling gigs for her. But for now, I was content to lie in that bed and stare up through the open roof at the stars in the clear sky.

"I don't want to leave," she said, the warmth of her breath grazing my bare chest.

"Me either, sir. Means we gon' have to put on clothes."

She laughed. "I really love you; you know that?"

"I love you so much, the shit hurts, sir."

TWENTY-EIGHT

ELLA

"Daughter! It's so good to see you! You look well!" Mother Erica gushed. It had been months since I'd seen my counselor's face. This woman and her staff at the Sankofa Holistic Healing Center saved me, restored much of my belief in myself, and gave me the fuel to move forward. We texted often but she'd requested this video call shortly after Armand and I returned from the Maldives.

"Thank you. You look beautiful, as always," I said, and she did, as regal as ever in a head wrap and matching caftan. She was an aging actress who appeared ageless.

"The ancestors are good to me. I can't deny that, and I can see they're being good to you, as well."

"I believe they are," I agreed. "Things are good. *I'm* good, happy."

"And in love? It's written all over you, daughter. Are you holding to what you learned here? Using all your tools?"

Resting against the back of the chair I was sitting in, I said, "I sure am."

ARMAND

"When you left me that message letting me know you needed to reschedule your appointment because you were going on a vacation, I was a bit surprised," Mr. Charles said.

Giving him a lopsided grin, I replied, "Why? I don't seem like the vacationing type or something?"

"Well, in the past when we discussed things you enjoy doing and ways you relax, you didn't mention traveling."

I shrugged. "I don't know. I travel so much for work, it gets old. But this was different. This was...special."

"You traveled with the young lady you told me about? The one you've been exploring kink with?"

"Yeah. Can I ask you something?"

"Of course."

I leaned forward on the loveseat in his office, my eyes on the floor. When I looked back up at him, I posed, "Do you think someone like me, with my past and issues, can love someone the right way?"

"How would you define the right way?"

"I...without hurting her, even unintentionally, like with my mom. I don't ever want to hurt her."

"You have tools now, and you have the *desire* to be calmer, to think before acting. You have the power to be the man you want to be, and I believe you're him. You haven't had an episode of the magnitude you did before leaving Detroit since you've been seeing me."

"But I've wanted to. I've wanted to fuck a lot of people up."

"Ah, don't you see? You wanted to but you didn't act on that desire. Armand, you have a past that is wrought with trauma. You were forced to grow up too soon and you took on adult responsibilities as a child. None of that will change. The effects of it all are long-reaching and hard to overcome, but *you're doing it.* You just have to keep doing the work. You simply cannot give up on yourself."

Nodding I agreed with, "Yeah...yeah."

"NATE! MAN, YOU'RE LATE!"

As we half-hugged, he said, "I got lost. I'm not from here. Man, whose house is this? What does this woman of yours do for a living because—"

He was looking past me when he cut his statement off, and I knew why.

I dropped a hand on his shoulder and said, "Nate, you know Ella, right?"

Ella stepped forward wearing a loose white dress and a smile, hugging Nate. "Of course he knows me. He's married to my cousin!"

When Ella ended the embrace, Nate just kind of stood there in obvious shock for a moment before finally saying, "Uh...wow. So, you two are..."

Grinning, I wrapped my arm around Ella and kissed her cheek. "We are."

TWENTY-NINE

ARMAND

"Ella, I had no idea you could cook like this—stone crabs, churrasco...you did two of this fool's favorites well!" Nate observed as the evening wound down. "He loves Miami cuisine."

I shrugged with a grin. "I love Miami."

I was in a good mood anyway because I liked Nate, but the news he gave me about some potential endorsements had me pretty close to giddy. I never thought any company would want to partner with my crazy ass again. When I first got drafted into the league, I had a few deals but quickly fucked them up. I was a fighter in high school and college, but it seemed the pressure of being in the NBA had driven me completely over the edge, causing me to act up during games, on and off court. Hell, I punched an arena employee in the tunnel once for talking shit about my performance. And the women? Man, I was wilding for real!

"I knew it was a special night for Armand. Only the best for him. I even made peanut butter cookies," Ella replied.

"You did, s—Ella?" I was sounding like a kid, but her peanut butter cookies were like crack to me, just like her pussy.

Leaning in to kiss me, she said, "I did. Let me go get them."

She left the formal dining room, and I looked over at Nate who was staring at me with this serious look on his face. It was like he was reading me.

"What?" I asked.

His eyes shot to the doorway and back to me. "That chain. She collared you?"

Before I could try to answer him because *what the fuck*, Ella returned with the cookies and another kiss for me.

About twenty minutes later, I was walking Nate to his car when he said, "I shouldn't have asked you about the chain. I just... I'm proud of the changes you've made. If she has anything to do with it, I support what y'all have one hundred percent."

"Uh...thanks, but how...why'd you ask me that?" I solicited, still shook that he'd figured it out.

"Well, I've never collared my wife, unless you count her wedding ring."

"You...you and your wife?!"

He nodded. "We're not hardcore or strict with the Dom/sub roles, but we dabble."

"Damn, I never knew. How'd you figure it out about me and Ella?"

"The way you look at her, it's pure reverence. And her? The way she caters to you, dotes on you? That tells the tale. Plus, for someone who's into kink, it's easy to read between the lines. You look happy. Congrats, man, but know that once her family gets wind of this, especially Leland, it ain't gonna be pretty."

"I know, but I love her, and she loves me."

"I understand that, but you need to be ready. Remember how you told me you reacted to him and your mom? They're solid, so you obviously overreacted. Don't expect any less from her folks and be prepared to weather it if you really want her."

"I get your point. It was fucked up what I did and said back then, and I regret it now, but I'm ready for whatever."

"Good. Talk to you later, Daniels."

"Later."

ELLA

Nathan Moore was long gone, and Armand was on his knees in my kitchen, head lowered, hands bound behind his back, and his body beautifully naked as I washed dishes. Well, that was when I wasn't sucking his dick. At that moment, it was quiet save for the clanking of dishes and his jagged breathing.

"P-p-permission to speak, sir?"

"Not if you're going to ask me when I'm going to let you cum."

"N-no, sir. Not that."

"Okay..."

"Uh, shit...I forgot."

"No, you didn't. You we're going to ask when I was going to let you cum."

"Yeah."

"So you lied to me?"

"Yeah."

"Yeah, what?"

"Huh? Oh...sir!"

I stopped washing dishes, giving him my full attention. "You *want* me to punish you, don't you?"

He didn't smile, but his pretty eyes bore amusement.

In response, I wiped my hands, went over to him, and did my best to suck his soul out of his body, making him howl like a wounded dog.

. . .

"WHAT ARE you going to do when your family finds out about us, sir?" Armand asked as he stood in the bathroom while I toweled him off from our bath. "They ain't gonna like it, considering my past."

"I know, but I love you. That's all that counts."

"Okay..." It was silent before he added, "Sir."

"You think I would stop being with you because of my family?"

He shrugged as I squatted to dry his legs.

So I stopped what I was doing and stared up at him, saw the uncertainty on his face, and almost cried. "You are everything to me and I'd do anything for you. I love you, Armand. I truly do. I don't care what anyone has to say about it. *Anyone*."

He closed his eyes, and I saw the exact moment his tears began to fall. Standing, I dropped the towel and grabbed his face, kissing his tears. "I love you. I love you. I love you..." I repeated.

THIRTY

ARMAND

"Y'all *got* to be cheating! Ain't no way y'all keep beating me like this if you're playing fair!" I said, shaking my head.

Layla stood from the floor with her hands on her hips, giving me the duck mouth. "We ain't cheating! We're just better than you! You need to accept it." This girl was too much.

"Uh-huh. You might beat us one day, but I don't think so. We're really good at this because our dad is Leland McClain," Lil' Leland chimed in.

"Oh, is that right? Y'all agree with them?" I asked the twins, who each occupied one of my thighs. One was playing with my chain. The other was staring at my hair. I couldn't tell them apart. I didn't even try to.

In response, one smiled at me. The other said, "Red!" Evidently, they were learning their colors. I think they were like two? Who knows?

"All right, y'all. Stop harassing Armand. Go wash your hands.

It's time for lunch," our mom said, and the room quickly cleared out.

I chuckled. "They be ready to eat, huh?"

"Yep, just like their big brother."

That didn't seem weird to me anymore, the fact that I was their brother, so I said, "Yeah. Hey, Ma?"

She leaned against the doorframe. "Yes?"

"I'm...I'm sorry for how I acted after you and Leland got together. I'm sorry for hurting you then or ever. I'm just...sorry. I really am."

She smiled, although I could see the tears in her eyes from across the room. "And you're forgiven. Always."

Neither of us spoke for a moment before she offered, "You wanna have lunch with us?"

I shook my head. "Nah, I'm gonna go see Granny. Haven't visited her in a while. She called me this morning asking me to come over."

She nodded. "Okay. I'm sure she'll be calling me to brag about seeing you. Hey, I love you, Boogie."

"I love you, too, Ma."

ELLA

While Armand spent the day visiting his family, I spent the day hashing out the details of a deal with the *Glam On It* cosmetics company. It was for an ad campaign I would post to my IG account. Evidently, all the hate I was getting for "betraying" Jackson had shot my engagement through the roof and gained me more than ten-thousand new followers. Business was business, and according to them, popularity was popularity, even if it was infamy. I liked the idea of being an influencer. I believed it would foster the precious privacy I was clinging to.

I was sitting at the kitchen table jotting down ideas for posts when he made it home. I heard him enter and close the front door, but he didn't call my name as he usually would, and he didn't come into the kitchen. Frowning, I headed into the foyer to find him standing with his forehead against the front door.

"Armand?" I said, unsure if I should approach him. I'd never seen him like this.

Nothing from Armand.

"Baby?"

Still nothing.

I'd taken a step toward him when he finally turned around, frantically undressing and dropping to his knees. Then he sat up and dropped his head while stretching his arms toward me, wrists touching. "I been driving around for hours. I...*please*," he said, voice shaky, pleading.

I rushed toward him, dropping to the floor in front of him. "Armand, what's going on?"

"I...I need you. I need you to do what you do. I need to feel the pain and then I need to feel the comfort. Please, sir. Help me."

Lifting his chin, I looked into his eyes and saw nothing but agony, deep, raw hurt. I wanted to know who or what had hurt him, to avenge him. Most of all, I wanted to ease his pain.

Kissing him, I said, "Okay, baby. Okay."

ARMAND

I was facing the front door, my hands braced against it, my legs spread apart, my eyes tightly shut. My thoughts were noisy, cluttered, and disorganized as the threat of a blackout loomed over me like a cloud heavily burdened with potential precipitation. As I waited for her, anticipation commingling with thick anger, I tried to shut the thoughts down even as the palms of my hands curled into fists, even as my desire to destroy something, *anything*, clung to every cell in my body. I wasn't sure if I would make it. I didn't think I could fight it off much longer, so I found myself croaking, "Sir..."

The word had barely left my mouth when the leather tails of the flogger collided with the middle of my back, the sudden impact making me jump a little. It didn't hurt, or at least not yet. Ella always started with soft blows that increased in intensity. She had this sixth sense for knowing how many times to strike the same spot before moving to another. A second soft thwack landed. Then another...and another. I flattened my palms against the door again, bracing myself for more intensity and she didn't fail me. The blows came harder and faster to that spot.

Harder and faster.

Harder and faster...until I felt a warmth spread over me as the pain began to dull my senses and quiet my thoughts. The leather hit my back a couple inches to the left now. She didn't utter a word and neither did I, but I suppose no words were needed.

This went on, this impact play, until my knees were weak, my legs were trembling, and I barely remembered my own damn name.

Then I felt it, the beautiful feeling of her soft lips against my skin as she kissed my back, soothing my pain while at the same time healing my soul. She kissed and caressed, droplets of moisture soon joining her lips on my skin—tears.

"Ella," I whimpered. "Sir..."

"I love you. I love you, Armand. I love you so much," she cried. "Turn around, baby."

I spun on weak legs and yelped when she pushed me against the door and kissed me hard. Then she dropped to a squat, taking me in her mouth. The back of my head hit the door and my hands clutched the back of *her* head as I groaned, "Ella...Ella...Ella. I love you, too. I love you, too..."

She sucked wildly, head bobbing, suction immaculate as she unraveled me with her mouth. I moaned and cried real tears as my back vacated the door. I began to rock in and out of her mouth, soon advancing from a relaxed pace to a full-on frenzy as I grunted and groaned through clenched teeth.

After I finally erupted, I crumpled to the floor and wailed as she held me in her arms.

THIRTY-ONE

ARMAND

Three hours earlier...

"Hey, Granny," I said as my grandmother opened her arms, welcoming me into the same house she'd lived in since I could remember. I'd offered to buy her another one, but she loved the place, so instead, I paid it off for her.

"Hey, baby! You look so good!" she cooed, backing up and cradling my face in her hands.

"Thank you. So do you."

"No I don't," she said with a chuckle. "I see you been staying out of trouble..."

"I been trying to."

"Come on and sit down so we can talk."

I took a seat on her floral sofa as she dropped into her recliner with an "Oomph!"

"You been feeling all right, Grandma? You keeping your sugar under control?" I asked.

"I been doing fine, baby. Just fine. I heard you been spending time with your little brothers and sister," she responded.

"Yes, ma'am. They're cute. Funny, too."

"They are, they are."

"You and my mom get along better now, huh? You be talking to her and stuff?"

"I do. She did good getting with Leland. He's a wonderful man."

I nodded.

Through a sigh she said, "Well, baby...the reason why I wanted to see you is because your other grandmother called me yesterday."

I frowned. "What other grandmother?"

"Joy Daniels, Malcolm's mother."

My stomach dropped. "My *father* Malcolm?" I knew Joy, kind of, so I knew she was referring to my father, but still...*what*?

She nodded.

"What she want? I heard he was getting out the pen soon. He need some money or a place to stay? Well, I told his folks the last time they tried that, that the only thing I'ma give him is what he gave me—not shit other than his raggedy-ass last name." The simple thought of that man and his grimy audacity had me ready to undo all the work I'd done over the past few months. My act-right was a centimeter from jumping out the window. To try and not wreck my grandmother's house, I started rubbing my hands over the thighs of my sweats.

"He *did* get out about a week ago, but she wanted you to know he passed away a couple days later. Someone shot him and left him for dead. She identified him but said they'll only release the body to his next of kin—you."

The room began to spin, and my head started feeling light.

Breathe.

Breathe.

Breathe.

Breathe, Daniels!

I managed to coach myself back from the edge, shifting my attention from where I'd been staring out her big picture window to her face, to see concern etched all over it.

"How'd she get your number?" I asked evenly.

"Uh...I used to go to church with one of her sisters. She gave it to her," she supplied, appearing nervous.

I nodded slowly. "And you have her number?"

"It's in my phone."

"Can you call her for me?"

"Why don't I just give you her number and—"

"No, ma'am. I don't want her number. I just need you to call her for me...please." My voice was low and soft. I swear I was trying not to fucking explode in my granny's living room. I was really, *really* trying. God knows I was.

"Okay, baby," she agreed. I left my seat as she dialed the number, was standing next to her when she said, "Hey, Joy. This is Diana. Boogie is here and he wants to speak with you."

After she handed me the phone, I lifted it to my ear. "Hello?"

"Armand?" my other grandmother said, her voice familiar and irritating as shit to me.

"Yeah, this me."

"Honey, did you hear about your father?"

Squeezing my eyes shut, I replied, "Mmhmm."

"I went down to the place and identified him...my poor baby. It's a damn shame how whoever shot him left him like an animal, like he wasn't nothing."

He wasn't, I thought, but said, "My Granny Diana said you need me to do something?"

"Yes, baby...they say only the next of kin can claim the body. That's you since you his only child. When can you go down there and do it? We need to lay him to rest. I know you'll probably want to pay for the funeral, won't you?"

"*Hell* no," I bit out.

"What?"

"I said *hell...no*. Your son will rot in that morgue before I even *consider* claiming his sorry-ass, deadbeat-ass, abusive-ass, jailbird-ass body, and I will cut my right arm off before I pay for his funeral! Fuck him and fuck you! Fuck y'all whole damn family! Don't ever ask me for shit again!"

I handed my shocked-into-silence grandmother her phone and left.

THIRTY-TWO

ARMAND

Now...

"Here, drink some more," Ella said, handing me the bottle of water I'd been sipping on.

"Okay...sir," I replied, my voice trembling. I was coming down from the scene, and I was exhausted, wrung out like a motherfucker. "Thank you."

"You know how I am about water. You sweat so much; I don't want you to get dehydrated."

"Not just for the water, for...for everything, sir."

She smiled. "When you feel stronger, we can take a bath. Just relax."

"My father died," I blurted as she moved to leave the bed where I was cocooned in a soft blanket.

She moved closer to me. "What?"

"My father died. Last week..." I went on to explain the whole claiming his body debacle.

"And you said no?"

"I said *hell* no...and fuck her and fuck him, and I meant it. He was nothing to me just like I was nothing to him. It's just..."

"The audacity of his family to ask that of you? The nerve of them to think you'd do that for a complete stranger? I get it. Family can be worse than an enemy. You did what was right for you and I don't see a damn thing wrong with it."

I fixed my eyes on her for more than a minute before reaching for her and pulling her close. "I love you, sir. Thank you."

"You are so welcome, baby. You are so welcome. *Always* welcome."

I WOKE up the next morning to find breakfast on the bedside table next to me and notifications making my phone buzz almost constantly. I headed to the bathroom to take a piss, returning to sit on the side of the bed. After I'd shoved a whole strip of bacon in my mouth, I checked my phone. Grandmother Joy had been talking to the blogs, letting them know how her rich, NBA-playing grandson was refusing to bury his father. Maybe she didn't follow my career or the shit I did on and off the court that had folks deeming me troubled and violent and unpredictable, but if she thought she could shame me into doing something, she was deadass wrong. I was the poster child for not giving a fuck and everyone knew it. I didn't have a reputation that could be tarnished. I'd wrecked it myself a long time ago.

ELLA

"You sure about this, sir?" he asked, his round, hazel eyes full of concern. "I'm good with whatever. I just don't want you to be harassed any more than you already are. Them 'On One for life' fools are nuts. I fight every day not to start hunting those muhfuckas down and fucking them up!"

"Okay, first of all, you can't fuck that many people up. Second, yes...I'm sure. You're mine. I'm tired of no one knowing it," I said.

He stared at the picture I was about to post for the *Glam On It* partnership. In it, I appeared to be gazing into a mirror, applying eyeshadow. Armand was sitting next to me kissing my cheek. We wore matching white, resort-style robes, my hair was in curlers, and Armand was...*Armand*-chest exposed, stubble on his face, his growing locks tied in a ponytail. For a photo taken in my house with a ring light and digital camera, it looked pretty damn good.

When Armand's eyes left the photo and found my face, there was so much emotion in them. Armand was profoundly complex, while at the same time, being surprisingly uncomplicated. The pain he carried was layered, but the cure was simple—love. With every act of love I offered him, I could see his trauma being dismantled. The same applied for me. His love, acceptance, and respect for me were the polar opposites of what Jackson had offered. I loved Armand so much for that, enough to deal with the hate, the anger, and the resistance, even if it came from my family.

"ELLA, pick up the phone! I don't know if that picture is fake or not, but it better be!" That was a direct quote from a voicemail left by my father.

"Ella, is that Armand in that picture you posted? What he doing with you?" That message was from Uncle Leland.

"El! Why y'all gotta look so sexy! Both of you! Damn!" I had to laugh at that message from Carlos.

"Ella, please call me back. I'm your mother, and whatever you think of me, I love you. Darling, please call mummy back." That was...well, you know.

"Hey, sweetie. You two look great together. I love it!" That was the beautiful Kim McClain.

"Hey, Ella. Please call your dad back. He's about to stroke out thinking that picture is real." Jo lowered her voice and added, "Very smart marketing, though. That photo is all over social media."

And on and on it went. My family was blowing my phone up and I wasn't answering, not yet, and not just because I was lying in bed with my body against Armand's, my face buried in his hard chest.

"I wanna call you Boogie," I said into said chest, kissing it.

"Shiiiid, you could call me 'that nigga' and I'd grin every time you said it, sir. You own me, remember?" he rumbled.

I smiled. "My family is losing their shit over that picture. They're tryna figure out if it's real."

"Yeah, my mom said Leland's been tryna get my number from her. She won't give it to him."

"Your mom is cool, always has been."

"Yeah, she is."

I kissed my way up from his chest to his neck to his chin, finally reaching my destination, his delicious lips. "You really never take this chain off," I observed, dipping down to kiss his neck again.

"And I never will."

ARMAND

"Where'd you say you were going?" I asked into the phone.

"Nowhere, really. Just driving around scouting possible locations for a photo shoot. Remember, I told you *Glam On It* wants to shoot content of us for their website since our pic went viral. They're willing to come here," Ella explained.

"Yeah, but can't they do that? I don't like you being out by yourself. I know you don't want to deal with a bodyguard, but them On One fans are stupid and they're everywhere."

"I'm not wearing makeup, I'm dressed like a stud, and I have on shades. No one will recognize me."

I smiled as I shook my head. "Be careful."

"I know you're at the Cyclones complex, so I'ma let the omitted sirs slide. Love you. Talk to you later."

"Love you, too."

"Was that my niece?"

Leland McClain scared the shit out of me, almost made me jump off that weight bench. I was trying to get a workout in since I'd been slacking, all wrapped up in my sir.

"Ain't you got a whole gym at your house? What you doing here?" I countered.

Standing over me, he asked, "What you doing taking pictures with my niece?"

I stood, although my stepfather still towered over my six feet and four inches. "What you doing having babies with my mama?"

"She's my wife! You saying you're married to Ella?" Dude sounded like he was about to steal on me.

"What I'm saying is I'm grown, Ella is grown, and me taking a picture or anything else with her is *our* business, not yours."

"Motherfucker!"

He grabbed me by the collar of my t-shirt, and I raised both my hands. "McClain, man...you don't want this. You bigger but I'm crazier. On the real, I'm fucking *insane*."

"Whoa, whoa, whoa! The fuck is going on?! McClain, how you gonna ask the whole team to be cool with dude and you doing this?" Polo Logan said. Ole boy came out of nowhere, but if anyone could pull McClain off me, it was Logan's huge ass.

He did, snatching McClain backward and telling me, "Get out of here, man. The team don't need this shit," while McClain tried to get out of his grip.

I nodded and left. Oddly enough, I really didn't want to fight McClain. I *would* and I *could*, but I honestly didn't want to.

THIRTY-THREE

ARMAND

It was after dark, and Ella wasn't home. One thing I knew about her was she was a homebody, a result of having spent her upbringing on a reality show. She loved modeling but no longer craved the spotlight. On One's ass had a lot to do with that too, though. She also wasn't answering her phone and I was getting more than a little worried.

I could get in my truck and try to find her, but I had no idea where she was scouting locations. I had to do something, nonetheless, because I was about to lose my complete shit.

Picking up my phone, I dialed her number again, foot tapping and heart galloping. Where the fuck was she?

The "hello" wasn't from Ella, so I took the phone from my ear to make sure it was her number I'd called and not some random white woman's. It *was* Ella's number, the one programmed in my phone as "Sir."

"Who the fuck is this?!" I barked. "And where the fuck is

Ella?!" I was on my feet now, although I didn't know where I was going.

"Oh, my! Um, I'm Wendy, a nurse at University Hospital. There's been an accident..."

THIRTY-FOUR

ELLA

Two hours earlier...

I was done scouting locations, having taken tons of pictures with my phone. I was sure to evade the areas Boogie told me to avoid but did venture into his old hood to get him one of those St. Paul sandwiches he was always raving about and a bag of Red Hot corn chips. It had been a good day despite my phone constantly ringing like I was working at a call center. I didn't silence it in case Boogie called me and I couldn't block my family. So I just ignored the calls, even the ones from my agent. Partnership offers were pouring in, but I wasn't in a rush to accept any of them. I liked the slower pace my life had settled into.

I couldn't wait to get back home to my man. I loved me some him for real, but the best part was that he loved him some me for real.

I was making one last stop at a gas station to fill up my tank in what would be deemed a good part of town when it happened.

First, I could feel eyes on me. I initially thought I was imagining it, but when I looked up, there actually was a guy staring at me. He was a couple stalls over, pumping gas. His glare was stapled to me, making my skin crawl. So, I shifted my gaze back to my pump and chided myself for taking my sunglasses off. My tank wasn't full, but something told me to stop the pump and leave. I was replacing the nozzle on its hook/hanger thing when a voice startled me due to its proximity to me. Snapping my head around, I came face to face with the guy who'd been staring at me. I mean, he was literally in my personal space.

Before I could think through what was going on, he spoke. "*I was with her for eternity. Never expected her to turn on me. Gave my heart to a straight gangster but I still can't find it in me to hate her!*" He was quoting lyrics from one of Jackson's songs, one written and recorded before we got together.

"On One for life!" he added.

I didn't notice the cup he was holding until he'd lifted it and dashed its contents in my face, making me yelp.

Then he yelled, "Fucking bitch!" as I gasped for air, my eyes burning from what I now recognized as liquor.

As he headed back to his vehicle, I could hear laughter, male laughter, coming from...somewhere. I didn't take the time to figure out who or where they were as I fumbled with the door handle, climbing into my vehicle and locking the doors. I should've called someone—the police? Armand, maybe? But I wasn't thinking clearly. I was in fight or flight mode, and I wasn't about to try to fight a man. My hand shook as I pushed the button to start my engine. My eyes still stung as I pulled away from the gas station. Then the tears started falling, further blurring my vision. I was so damn scared and disoriented that I'm not even sure how I ended up hitting that pole, but I did.

THIRTY-FIVE

ARMAND

Now...

"There's been a what?" I asked. I was heading out the door now, my heart slamming against my rib cage, ominous thoughts blaring in my brain.

"An accident. A car accident," the voice on the other end of the phone said. She said she was a nurse at a hospital. Ella was in the hospital?

"Ella was in an accident? She's there now?" I didn't have my fucking keys. I was outside but my keys were in the house.

"Yes, she is. I was going to try to find an emergency number in her phone, but there's a lock code. Then you called. Are you her next of kin, or can you contact them to let them know she's here?"

"She's in the emergency room?" I asked as I rushed back in the house through the unlocked front door.

"Yes, are you—"

I hung up, frantically searching the room for my keys before realizing they were in the pocket of my sweatpants. I pulled them out and fell to my knees on the floor, dropping my head. She wasn't okay. If she was, she'd be in possession of her own phone, and she would've answered it or called me.

She wasn't okay.

I couldn't take this shit. I needed to get to the hospital, to her, but I couldn't move. She was my strength. How the fuck was I supposed to be strong if she wasn't okay?

I don't think I had a conscious thought to call her, but I did. Somehow, I managed to make the call, and when I heard my mother say, "Hey, Boogie," in this bright voice, I let out a groaned, "Mama, I need help!"

MY MOTHER PICKED me up from Ella's and took me to the hospital. I said thank you when I slid in the vehicle, but we didn't talk on the ride there because I couldn't. I was both too deep in my thoughts and muzzled by fear. She had to pat my arm to let me know we'd made it. In response, I jumped, my eyes wildly shifting from the nothingness I'd been focusing on, to her face, to the other side of the windshield.

I'd grabbed for the door handle when she said, "Boogie, wait."

Snatching my head around, eyes wide, I gave her my attention.

"I told Leland. I called him shortly after I left home. I also called my mother. She's on her way over there to watch your siblings," she informed me.

"He's on his way up here?" I mumbled, opening the door.

"Yes, and he called Big South," she continued.

I didn't mean any disrespect, but I didn't have time for a breakdown of who called who. Ella was in that hospital hurt, possibly severely injured. My damn sir, the most powerful person I knew, the only person in the world I'd crawl across hot coals for, couldn't even talk to me on the phone. I needed to get inside that hospital immediately. Fuck everything else.

So, as I climbed out the vehicle, I offered my mom another "thank you" and took off toward the ER entrance.

"Boogie! Armand! Slow down!" my mother's voice called after me. I would've slowed down if I could've. Didn't she realize that?

The ER waiting room was a blur of faces and sounds and light as I approached some lady at a desk and breathlessly blurted, "Ella McClain. She's here. I need to see her."

I felt a hand on my arm, looked down to see my mom's worried face, and turned back to the lady.

"Yes, she's here—"

"I know that! I need to see her!" I boomed.

"Boogie, calm down," my mother pleaded.

The woman gave me a hard look before saying, "You'll have to take a seat while I see what's going on with her. She can't have visitors right now."

"What?!" I was a microsecond from wrecking that whole damn building at that point.

"Boogie, do you wanna get kicked out? Arrested? If you want to see her, come sit down with me," my mother reasoned.

I glared at the woman before the word *counterintuitive* popped into my head. Ella was hurt, but if I got myself together and waited, I'd get to see her. If I got kicked out, I wouldn't. So I sat my ass down.

"THANK YOU, MAMA," I nearly whispered as I stared straight ahead.

"You already thanked me for picking you up and you're more than welcome," she replied.

I turned and looked at her sitting beside me in the waiting area before leaning in to kiss her cheek, making her smile.

Some time had passed, and I was leaned forward, elbows on my knees, eyes on the floor, when I heard Leland's voice. "So you snuck out the house without security to pick him up and bring him here?"

"Exactly," my mom said. "He has a right to be here. This is not a fight you want to start with me, Leland. Sit down. We're waiting to hear what's going on with Ella."

I didn't raise my head but figured he'd obeyed her since he didn't say anything else. Good, because if he got down wrong with my mama, I was going to fuck him up.

Time was moving way too slowly, but eventually, the lady at the desk said something that included Ella's name. I jumped up, the only thing in my line of vision the person who'd said my sir's name.

I didn't realize my mom and Leland were behind me until Leland spoke. "Is she okay?"

"Can you all come with me, please?" This came from a lady in scrubs. I didn't notice her until she spoke, either. Damn, I was totally fucked up in the head.

I'd opened my mouth to protest when my mom grasped my hand and said, "Come on, Boogie."

I glanced at her, my eyes still wild as I nodded in agreement.

HER INJURIES WERE due to the airbag deploying—lacerations to her face, contusions to her chest and arms, a fractured right arm, left wrist, and nose, a concussion, and irritated lungs caused by chemicals released with the airbag.

The woman—a doctor—kept talking, and I listened, trying to absorb it all. Trying to understand.

"She was unconscious when she arrived, but she's awake now. There doesn't seem to be any cognitive issues."

I heard Leland say something, but I couldn't focus on it. "Can she have visitors?" I asked. All I cared about was seeing her.

"In a few minutes. I believe they're in the middle of doing an ultrasound right now."

I frowned. "A what? What's that for?"

"Oh, shit," my mother muttered.

"We're just making sure everything's okay with the baby," the doctor said.

THIRTY-SIX

ARMAND

Ella is pregnant?

That thought repeated in my head.

Ella is pregnant?

I knew it was mine. That wasn't even a question in my mind, but how? She had an IUD. I knew that for a fact, so *how*? Would she want the baby? Did *I* want a baby?

Her baby?

Hell yeah!

Ella is pregnant.

The doctor was gone. My mom and Leland were talking, getting louder and louder, and I just stood there staring at the space the doctor had vacated.

Ella was pregnant.

And hurt.

I needed to see her.

Turning, my gaze collided with Leland's. Yanking himself free from my mother's grip, he flew into my face, voice low. "I need to be here for my niece, so I'm fighting the desire to kick your ass like a motherfucker, but this shit you pulled with her, this revenge? Best believe you gon' pay!"

"Leland, stop! What the two of them have has nothing to do with us, just like what we have has nothing to do with them!" my mother chastised.

As for me, I was dealing with too many emotions to utter a word. Instead, I walked back over and reclaimed my abandoned seat, my eyes on the floor, my head throbbing, my heart aching.

Ella is pregnant.

"McClain family!"

I was up on my feet so fast I nearly fell. All three of us—Leland, my mom, and I—rushed to the owner of a new voice...a nurse. "Ms. McClain can have a visitor now."

"I'm her uncle, her next of kin. I'll go first," Leland said.

I didn't give a fuck if he was an exact DNA match to her. I was going to see her first. I was just about to tell him that when the nurse advised, "She's asking for an Armand. She says she only wants to see Armand."

ONE OF HER eyes was swollen shut. Dried blood, bruises, and cuts covered her face. Her lip was busted, and as she looked up and saw me approaching her, she began to cry while reaching for me.

I rushed to the side of the gurney, grasping her outstretched hand and leaning in close to her face. "Hey, I'm here. I'm here, sir," I softly said. "I'm here."

Her words were garbled as she spoke, but I could understand her. "Everything hurts, Boogie. Everything hurts," she cried.

"I'm sorry. I'm so sorry this happened to you." I gently rested my forehead against hers and closed my eyes. I wanted to cry, too, but I fought it. She didn't need to see me crumble.

"I'm pregnant," she whispered.

"I know. We'll talk about it later. Just...just calm down. I'm here, and I ain't going nowhere."

"Okay..." she sobbed.

ELLA

"Miss McClain, they have a bed for you upstairs. We're going to move you within the hour."

I blinked slowly and then attempted to focus the eye that wasn't swollen shut. It was no use, so I just nodded at the blurry blob before me.

"Sir...can I ask you to leave and meet us upstairs? Her room number will be—"

"No," I interrupted her. "He stays."

"Um, okay. Your other family can meet you upstairs then. Your, uh, father is here," she said.

"Okay," I replied.

"I could just meet you upstairs," Armand offered after the nurse left.

"I don't want you to. I can't...I want you with me. Okay? Please stay with me."

"I ain't going nowhere. I promise."

I DON'T REMEMBER FALLING asleep but found myself waking up in a different location. I was no longer in the ER but in a room. I could feel Armand to my right. I could smell him, too. Not sweat or cologne, just *him*. His was an aroma I'd memorized. There was someone else in the room, too, someone whose energy I knew well, an energy that comforted me as much as Armand did.

"Daddy?" I rasped.

I heard movement as a familiar bulky frame approached me.

"Princess, I got here as soon as I could. Lil' Ev has the flu or else Jo would be here, too. I was so worried about you..."

"Uh...I'll leave so you two can talk," Armand offered.

"Yeah, you do that," Daddy bit out, "and when me and my daughter are done talking, I'ma take care of your ass! You 'bout to dissa-fucking-pear, my nigga!"

"Daddy!" I shrieked.

"Man, look—" Armand tried, but my dad interrupted him.

"*Man, look* my ass! I knew something was up when I saw you sniffing in behind her at your mom's party. Shoulda handled your ass then. I don't know who the fuck told you that you could mess with my damn baby girl and live, but they misinformed you! I'm about to fucking end your little ass!"

"Daddy, stop!" I yelled. "Stay, Armand. Daddy, I'm glad you're here, but please don't talk to him like that. He doesn't deserve it. He's done nothing wrong."

My dad shook his head. "This ain't right, Ella."

"Me being hurt isn't right. Me and Armand? That's the rightest thing in my life. Didn't you tell me to move on, to live?"

"Not with this motherfucker! Princess, you're pregnant?" my dad asked, sounding pained. "By *him*?"

"Yes, and I'm twenty-three, and he didn't take my virginity. He didn't take anything from me I wasn't willing to give."

"Shit," Armand muttered. "Ella, I don't mind stepping out—"

"No!" I nearly shouted.

"Okay, I'ma just stay my ass right here then." Armand muttered from where he was still seated beside me.

"Daddy," I began, shifting my attention to him, "I know you feel like I'm still your little girl—"

"That's not it. I realize you're an adult now, but you've been sheltered. I don't trust him with you. I don't want you hurt," my father cut in.

"He'd never hurt me, and I'm not as sheltered as you think," I countered.

"No cap," Armand mumbled.

My dad shot him a look and grunted, "Ella, I know you think you know him but—"

"I love him," I said, making him fall silent. "I don't *think* I love him, I don't *believe* I love him, I *know* I love him just like I *know* he loves me. The beef he had with Uncle Leland? His reputation? Whatever he did in the past to whoever doesn't matter to me. I love the Armand Daniels that *I* know. I'm carrying that Armand Daniels' baby. You're gonna have to accept that and him if you want to remain in my life and my baby's life because he isn't going anywhere unless I tell him to. Right, Armand?"

"Whatever you say," Armand agreed.

"And I'm not ever going to tell him to leave me," I finished. Yeah, I was a McClain, but I was also a Reese. I could be a bitch when I needed to. Armand was mine and no one was taking him from me.

THIRTY-SEVEN

ELLA

Armand was literally vibrating as he paced my hospital room, his anger thick and palpable. If I didn't know it wasn't directed toward me, I might've been afraid.

Instead of helping me, someone had recorded the incident at the gas station and posted the video on social media. The upside was an arrest had been made. The downside? Armand had watched the video repeatedly and an arrest wasn't good enough for him.

"I need to kill him," he growled. "They gon' let him out after little to no time so he can do this shit again. If I kill him, the world will be rid of him."

"And I won't have you. Neither will the baby," I advised.

He stopped in his tracks, the hum of his anger dissipating as he approached me.

"Sit down, Boogie. Talk to me."

He took his seat, the one he'd been sleeping in for two days while they ran tests on me, casted my arm and wrist, and removed my IUD. Evidently, it had shifted into my cervix, which was how I got pregnant.

"You really want to keep the baby?" he asked softly.

ARMAND

"The odds of a woman getting pregnant with an IUD in place are less than one percent, so this baby is meant to be. Besides, it's yours. Of course I do," she assured me. "Do...you want to keep it?"

Fixing my eyes on her, I said, "It's yours. Of course I do...sir."

She smiled.

She was seven weeks, and so far, the gynecologist believed the baby would be fine and so would Ella with time to heal.

I lightly rested a hand on her stomach. "I love you, sir."

"I love you, too," she replied. "I'm down both arms. It'll be a while before we can play."

"I don't care. I'ma take care of you until you heal. We got the rest of our lives to play." I stood, leaning in to kiss her. I was just backing away from her when her phone rang. Grabbing it from the over-bed table, I checked the screen. "It says Unc," I informed her with wrinkled brows.

She nodded, and once I accepted the call, she said, "Hello?"

A man I'd later learn was her great Uncle Lee Chester's voice boomed from the phone's speakers as it lay on the table. "Niece! I heard you got in a wreck!"

"Yes, sir. I'm okay now, though," she replied with a smile.

"They tell me you fractured your arm and shit. Glad you ain't break nothing! Look, I really called because I heard you done got knocked up by my Kimmy's son. Uh...that boy they call Armor All."

"Armand?" she squeaked.

I mumbled, "The fuck?"

"Naw, they call him something else, don't they? Booger! That's it. You done got knocked up by a nigga named Booger?"

The fuck, squared?

"Uh..." Ella said. I could see why she was lost for words.

"Looka here, ain't none of this my business, but I just wanna say, if he come from my Kimmy, he all right with me. Just don't name that baby Booger Junior, okay?" her uncle advised.

I could tell she was fighting hard not to laugh and so was I, although I was also battling to maintain my frown.

"Okay, Unc," she managed to say.

"All right, niece...Lou wanted some ribs, but it's raining down here, so I brought the grill inside. 'Bout to fire it up!"

The fuck cubed?

"Oh, is that safe, Unc?" Ella asked.

"Naw, no steaks. Just ribs. I'ma check on you later, niece," he said and ended the call.

Ella and I stared at each other and then fell out laughing.

AFTER FIVE DAYS, they were finally letting Ella go home. I was so happy I didn't know what to do! I was tired of sleeping in that chair, or *trying* to sleep in that chair, but I would've slept there every night for a year if I needed to. It would've taken the jaws of life to pry me from her bedside. Thankfully, my mom brought me some clothes and stuff, so I wasn't sitting around being funky and shit, but I was glad we were getting to leave.

I was bent over her bed, a hand on each rail as I leaned in to kiss her and kiss her and kiss her. Her face looked better, still scuffed up, but better. She had casts on both arms and bandages on her nose, little Band-Aids on her cheeks and forehead, but I swear she was still the most beautiful woman I'd ever laid eyes on.

One last kiss and I smiled into her eyes. "This, *us*, it's crazy. I had the biggest crush on you for the longest. I'd look at your pics on IG and think *damn, she's fine.* I just knew you had some good pussy."

Grinning up at me, she asked, "And?"

I smirked. "I let you collar me. *Me*, Armand DeShawn 'I kicks ass for breakfast' Daniels. That oughta tell you your pussy is un-fucking-rivaled, incomparable, unmatched."

She laughed. "You're stupid. Hurry back."

"I will. I'm just gonna pull my truck around. Scotty was clutch for driving it here for me yesterday."

"Yeah."

I reluctantly left her room, nodding at the muscle Big South was paying to stand outside her door. I'd made it into the elevator and was watching the doors slide closed when a big hand stopped them. They slid open to reveal Big South, one of his enormous-ass bodyguards, and Leland.

Shit.

I dropped my head and sighed as they filed into the box. They'd left me alone after Ella set her dad straight, not exactly being friendly, but not harassing me, either. I guess that shit was over.

When I lifted my head, I found all angry eyes on me. "Three on one, huh? All y'all bigger than me. You must really think I can box to be bringing backup."

"I'm not planning to fight you. We need to talk," Big South said. Dude was fucking gargantuan, not only in stature but his presence. Full disclosure, I was a fan of his, but if he thought he was going to talk me out of Ella's life? Well, *fuck that.*

"Y'all brought a bodyguard just to talk to me?" I questioned.

"We brought a bodyguard because he's Big South and a motherfucker shot at me one time. Not to mention your recent past reputation. We ain't stupid," Leland said.

I nodded as the elevator stopped on a lower floor. The doors slid open, and a white lady looked inside. Her eyes ballooned before she let them close. I guess we *were* a menacing sight.

"I'm going to get my truck so I can take Ella home. Y'all welcome to walk and talk," I offered.

They followed me to my truck, but no one spoke until I hit the button on the key fob to unlock the doors.

"Let's talk in there," Big South said, nodding at my vehicle.

I shrugged. "Get in, then."

My ass had barely touched the driver's seat when Big South, who'd slid in on the passenger side, gripped me by the neck and got all up in my face. "Listen, little nigga, I don't know who the fuck you think you are, but that girl up there in that room? She is my fucking heart, my *Princess*. There ain't a thing in this world I won't do for her. Do you understand?"

I just stared at his ass because how was I supposed to talk while he was legit choking me out?

"Ev," Leland said, "you choking him. He can't talk."

"Good," Big South growled, "because I was just about to tell him if he ever even dreams about putting his hands on my Ella, he will fucking evaporate and I know someone who can make it happen."

"He ain't lying," Leland added.

Big South let me go and I shook my head. I wanted to rub my neck, but I wasn't going out like that. Still, I couldn't help but be a little out of breath as I said, "You tryna protect her from me when I would beat my own ass before I hit her, but you let On One treat her like shit. He used to hit her, you know that? He used to talk crazy to her. She's been keeping it a secret because all y'all, the whole world, love his ass so much, but she was miserable with dude. I love her. Shit, on the real, I damn near worship her, and Ella is the one running things with us. She says jump, and I don't even ask how high. My ass just jumps and hope it's high enough. You can't see that?"

Big South just stared at me, but I could tell I was getting through to him.

"So you're talking shit about a dead man now?" Leland interjected.

"Nah, I'm telling the truth. If y'all know Ella like you think you do, you saw it. You might not have realized it at the time, but you saw it, and look, Leland, I know I acted a fool over you and my mom, but I thought I was protecting her from another asshole. I was wrong. I apologized to her, and now, I'm apologizing to you. I'm sorry for everything I said and did. I can see what y'all got is real, and just like I was wrong about y'all, y'all are wrong about us. I love Ella. No cap. I love her so much that even *I* don't understand it. I would never, *ever* hurt her. It's killing me that they locked that dude up before I could get to him. I *need* to fuck him up."

"I was gonna torture his ass, like cut him up or something," Big South said.

"Yeah, I was thinking the same thing," Leland agreed. "Cut him, burn him alive, something..."

"I was gon' cut his dick off and shove it down his got-damn throat after I cut his balls off and stuffed them in his ears," I told them. The truck fell silent as they stared at me. Then we all started laughing. Well, everyone except the bodyguard. I almost forgot his big ass was even there.

"Does he talk?" I asked.

"Who? Bear? Not unless I tell him to," Big South replied. "I brought him to be Ella's armor. Her hardheaded ass is going to have security every time she steps out the house from now on. I don't give a fuck if she steps out the door to look at the sun, he gon' be with her."

"Yeah, I told her that. She gonna mess around and make me do something to somebody that'll put me in jail. How I'ma take care of her if that happens?" I said.

Big South fell against the back of the seat and shook his head. "She's my baby, man...I can see that you love her, but shit! Just...be good to her, man. She's special. She's my princess."

"I can't be nothing but good to her. She's everything to me. She got my heart."

THIRTY-EIGHT

ELLA

It was taking forever for Armand to make it back to my room, and I was getting anxious, worried. What if one of Jackson's fans attacked him? What if they seriously hurt him? He didn't have a bodyguard, but we were going to have to rectify that for both of us. I'd definitely learned my lesson.

When my phone sounded, I carefully maneuvered my left hand, using the exposed fingers to move it closer to me on the over-bed table, tapping the screen to answer it and putting my agent on speakerphone.

"Hey, Shelly," I greeted.

"Hey, beautiful. Feeling any better?"

"Better than when you called an hour ago? No."

Shelly chuckled. "I'm worried about you is all."

"Don't be. I'm in good hands."

"Armand Daniels?"

"Yep," I said with a smile.

"You two? Now that's a real plot twist."

"Not really. You'd be surprised at how well we match."

"Hmm, well I actually called you for business this time. I know you've a long recovery ahead of you, so you don't have to do this now, but several reporters are asking to interview you and Armand about your relationship and your attack. So much is going on with fandoms right now. It's really a hot topic."

I stared at the phone for so long that Shelly said, "Just think about it. We can talk about it later."

"No," I said. "I'll do it, and the sooner the better. I want the world to see me, broken bones, bruises, and all; just make sure we get the best deal."

"Okay! I'll get on it!"

ARMAND WAS HELPING me into a wheelchair as we prepared to leave the hospital when the door opened. I looked up, and my face fell. I'd hoped she wouldn't make an appearance, but she was my mother. I suppose she felt obligated to come.

She looked beautiful, a mortified expression on her face. Beauty was very important to Esther Reese. It was, after all, the source of her well-being. My looks were important to me, too, but they weren't my identity. If my modeling career ended, it wouldn't destroy me. I could move on. I understood I was more than just a pretty face. Plus, my man was rich.

Sighing, I mumbled, "Fuck."

"What?" Armand said. His eyes found her and widened. "Oh. I didn't hear anyone come in."

Once I was in the wheelchair, I looked up at Armand. "Can you give us a few minutes?"

"You sure?" he asked.

"Yeah. Five minutes."

He nodded and left, taking all my joy with him.

She moved closer to me, her tall, thin frame covered in a bright yellow pantsuit, causing her flawless dark skin to glow. She was radiant, ageless, and the last person in the world I wanted to see.

She raised her hands to her mouth as she inched closer to me. "Oh, Ella...what have you done to yourself?"

I shook my head and chuckled bitterly. "Because I *tried* to run into a pole, right? Why are you here?"

Dropping her hands, she clasped them at her waist. "I wanted to see about you, dear. I was worried."

"Well, you can see I'm fine. So you can go now."

"Ella! When are you going to stop this? You've been acting out for so long. I miss my little girl."

"I'm not a little girl. I haven't been a little girl in a long time. You know when I stopped being a little girl? It started when it clicked in my head that you'd been using me to manipulate my father for years, starting with you convincing me that I wanted to be a part of your stupid reality show, but I came into full awareness when I realized you were using me to terrorize my dad and Jo, something you've not once apologized for! You've never apologized for *anything*!"

"Because none of it is true! It's simply not true! Anything I did was for you! I was merely trying to restore our family for *you*!"

I ignored those spoken delusions and continued with, "But I became a full-grown woman when Claude DuMont called me with a drunken confession five years ago about how he was my real father and not Everett McClain. That shit grew me up real quick!"

She gasped, her mouth hanging open.

"Yeah, *I know*. I know! Claude doesn't remember the conversation. He only knows he called me because he saw it on his phone, or at least that's what he told me. I've never bothered to jog his memory because it's not a conversation I want to have. Nevertheless, I *can't* forget, but him being my biological father makes sense. I don't look like my dad or anyone on his side of the family, but I am almost identical to Claude's mother, Laurette."

"Ella—"

"I know my daddy knows. That's why he's still so mad at you after all these years but let me tell you something. My father is Everett James McClain. *Period.* I will never bring this up to him and no one else will ever know. *No one.*"

"Ella, I didn't *try* to make someone else your father. I—"

"I don't care. Now, let's practice. Who is my father?" I asked, eyebrows lifted.

"Everett," she softly said.

"Exactly."

"Uh, it's been five minutes," Armand informed me, peeking his head in the door.

"I'm ready," I answered him. Then to my mother, I said, "Leave me alone. I mean it."

And I *did* mean it.

THIRTY-NINE

ELLA

"First of all, I want to thank you for allowing us into your lovely home to chat with you today. I know you're still recovering from your accident, so I'm sure this is not easy for you," Nevada Jamison, a reporter from BNN, the Black News Network, said. She was short and thin, wearing a gorgeous purple dress from one of Claude's past spring collections. I'd always liked her, so I chose her from amongst the throng of reporters and networks who'd contacted my agent.

I was dressed casually in jeans and a t-shirt, had opted to wear no makeup, and my hair was pulled back in a ponytail. This was me—real, raw, casts on each arm, a bandage on my nose, scratches on my face. Injured but not broken.

"No, it's not easy, but it's necessary. I want my voice to be heard. I want to finally share truths I had no business keeping secret in the first place," I replied.

"And you want to do it with him by your side?" Nevada asked.

I nodded, shifting my attention to Armand, who sat to my left with his arm around my shoulder, right by my side as he was when I was in the hospital. "Yes, with him."

Armand leaned in and kissed my cheek. "I love you," he said before lowering his gaze to the floor, his profile as beautiful as ever.

"I love you, too," I supplied softly.

"Well, I believe you two just confirmed your as-of-yet rumored relationship status," Nevada verbally surmised.

In response, I smiled.

"I see...well, let's get to the matter at hand," Nevada continued. "Ella, can you tell us what happened on the night of your accident?"

I did. As hard as it was, *I did.* I recounted everything and felt everything all over again—the fear, the liquor stinging my eyes, the disorientation, the impact, the pain.

"It may seem like nothing to some people. No, I wasn't sexually assaulted, and yes, I escaped with my life. It's not just about being confronted or assaulted the way I was, it's that no one helped. People laughed, people recorded with their phones, people uploaded the video and shared the footage, but no one helped me. The video allowed for the man to be found and arrested. I'm grateful for that, but it's not lost on me that it was shared because it was entertaining to people.

"I'm a person, a human with feelings. Yes, I grew up on camera and my parents are famous. I have a great career and a wonderful man who loves me, but I'm just a regular person with extraordinary people around me. I deserved better, and the fact that as a black woman, a black man did that to me? Well, that's especially egregious as far as I'm concerned."

"What about the tons of On One fans who feel you've betrayed him by moving on so quickly? His mother and sister have stated on numerous occasions that they feel you've turned your back on him and his legacy," Nevada posed.

Armand shifted on the sofa, blowing out a breath. I knew he wanted to jump in but was glad he didn't. *I* needed to do this.

"Nevada, On One was an incredible talent. That's undeniable. He was also kind and giving. He supported his family until the day he passed and even after," I supplied.

"Yes, some are speculating that him not including you in his will was a point of contention between you and his family," Nevada shared.

"That's not true. I wasn't married to him. I didn't expect to be in his will, nor did I have any desire to be. I genuinely cared for him and I believe he cared for me, but I need for people to understand that often what's portrayed publicly does not always align with reality. Our relationship was not perfect. By the end, it was not healthy and neither was On One."

"Are you saying he was ill?"

"I'm saying he was struggling with an addiction...to pills. I'm saying that to those who were in his inner circle, it was not a secret. I'm saying he wasn't always the kindest person *to me*. I'm saying he was human and flawed and at times...abusive."

Nevada's eyes widened. "Abusive toward you, Ella?"

I nodded, blinking back tears. "Yes, and those closest to him know I'm telling the truth. They witnessed it."

"These are serious allegations, *very* serious. On One's fans are already angry with you. This could serve to add fuel to that fire."

"It could and it probably will, but I have proof. Would you like to see?"

ARMAND

"I'll be glad when these casts come off. I know you're tired of having to do all this," Ella said, sounding frustrated.

"Nah, I like it. Helps me get to know you better, sir," I said as I placed a plate of food before her.

"Really?"

"Yeah. I've had to learn what you like to eat, your favorite soap, perfume, clothes. Before this, everything was about me."

"You've given me the gift of your submission. You! Why wouldn't it be all about you? Taking care of you is my top priority."

I stared at her for a moment. "I *gave* you my submission. I guess that's true."

"It is! You're the ultimate alpha male. You are so strong and powerful, intimidating as hell, and that doesn't change when we play. You school yourself *for me.* That is so precious to me. It... thank you."

I blinked and shook my head. "No, sir. Not today. You ain't about to make me cry in front of my son. Eat up," I said, holding a forkful of food up to her mouth.

"How many times do I have to tell you that I can feed myself?"

"I don't care. I like feeding you."

She took the bite and hummed with pleasure. "Mmmm, who told you I like curried goat, and where did you get it? Did you cook this?!"

"Your dad told me after I called and asked him for a list of your favorite foods. Chef Scotty cooked it."

Her eyes ballooned as she stopped chewing. "Oh! Thank him for me! And, uh...you've been talking to my dad?"

"Yeah, I mean, he still only refers to me as *Little Nigga*, but at least he ain't threatening my life anymore."

"I still can't believe he choked you..."

"I can. That's why I keep saying son, although we don't know yet. Because if it's a girl? I'ma fuck up any dude who looks at her. She better be a lesbian."

"You do know that lesbians use straps, right?"

"Well, she gon' be a non-fucking lesbian."

Ella rolled her eyes as I continued feeding her.

. . .

"AFTER OUR INTERVIEW CONCLUDED, Ella McClain showed me the video you are about to view. It was taken on her phone some months before rapper On One's death. I want to warn you that it is disturbing. If you are sensitive to violent content, you may not want to view this footage."

The image on the TV shifted from Nevada Jamison to an iPhone video taken in a hotel room. From what Ella told me, the phone was in her lap, facing up. At the time, she'd been filming a video for social media, something silly, when On One started an argument with her. Anyone who knew him or listened to his music knew it was definitely his voice. He was saying all kinds of shit, calling her names that made me want to dig his bitch ass up, resurrect him, and beat him back to death. Then he came into frame, towering over her. She was saying something to defend herself, nothing that should've motivated him to do what he did next, but he did it anyway. He spit in her face before punching her in the side of her head.

It was all I could do not to fuck Ella's TV up. Instead, I turned it off and began pacing the room. I had to calm down.

"Boogie, come here," she said.

I shook my head. "Give me a minute."

"It wasn't a request."

I stopped in my tracks and looked at her. Her face was blank.

"Come here...*now*," she ordered.

I nodded and obeyed. I was about to sit next to her on the sofa when she said, "No, stand in front of me."

I did.

"Let me see my dick."

"What...sir?"

"These casts come off next week and I swear I'm going to beat the shit out of you when they do if you don't take my dick out right now!"

I dropped my pants and underwear. Of course I was as hard as Mount Everest at that point.

I moaned as her tongue found the head of my dick.

"Did I ever tell you why I moved here to St. Louis?" she asked before taking me in her mouth, and she was doing this shit with no hands!

"Um...fuck! No, sssssir," I replied.

She let me slowly slide from her mouth. "I moved here because I knew you'd been traded to the Cyclones."

I frowned down at her. "What, sir?"

Taking me down her throat and popping me out, she released a breath and said, "You know how you said you had a crush on me? Well, I've had a crush on you, too. I'd watch your games, stalk your social media. I'd see you in pictures with women and wish I was them. You were so damn fine and mean and...I'd wonder how your body would feel between my legs, how your mouth would feel against mine, how your tongue would taste. Would your hands be rough when you touched me? Most of all, I wondered just how good it would feel for you to be inside me. I was sure you had good dick."

She was legit sucking my whole vocabulary from my brain when I somehow managed to ask, "*And*, sir?"

She didn't reply. Instead, she sucked and slurped and licked until she pulled my soul from my body. I was standing before her shivering and shit when she said, "And I was right. You got the *best* dick."

"S-s-sir, let's get m-m-m-married," I stammered, lowering my eyes to her face. She looked as high as I felt because Ella loved giving me head almost more than she loved *me*. I would've bet money that her panties were soaking wet at that moment. When her lips were swollen like they were now from pleasing me, she looked so lovely to me. Only a few weeks had passed, so her face still bore the evidence of the accident, but her beauty remained unmatched.

I watched as she dropped her gaze, and when she lifted her eyes to my face again, a single tear rolled down her cheek as she whispered, "Okay."

FORTY

ARMAND

My eyes were glued to the screen. I was glad Ella's casts were off so I could hold her hand because I needed her to ground me, to keep me from floating out of that room. I was truly happy, so happy that this all felt unreal. That was my baby on that screen—big head, tiny body, little legs and arms moving.

My baby.

"Here's the heartbeat," the tech pointed out, and all I could do was blink back tears. My baby had a heartbeat.

I felt Ella squeeze my hand before she asked, "What do you think?"

"I think...thank you, Ella. Thank you," I replied.

"Thank you back."

ELLA

"Today is the day, no? I am happy for you, chérie. I am happy that you are happy. I only wish..."

"Claude, please don't ruin this day for me by bringing her up. I love her as my mother, but I've made a choice not to have her in my life. You told me you would respect that. It was a requirement for me to continue with our friendship. I care for you, but I will cut you off, too, if you can't adhere to my boundaries."

"I can. I *will*. Forgive me, mon ange. I will not bring her up again. Congratulations."

"Thank you. Oh, I've gotta go."

"Okay, tout mon amour!"

I hung up as Aunt Kim entered my bedroom. "They're ready?" I asked with wide eyes. My heart was hammering in my chest.

Smiling, she nodded. "Yes, they are! You look beautiful, Ella!"

"Thank you. I've gained so much weight. I mean, I don't care about that, but I do hope this dress looks flattering. I don't want to look back on this day and think I should've chosen something else, something not so...fitted."

"Oh, no! That dress is gorgeous on you!"

Smiling, I asked, "How's Boogie?"

"Excited, nervous, happy, in love."

"Me, too."

"Ella, you ready—shit. Oh my god. Princess..." That was my dad. This was his first time seeing me in my dress, hence his reaction. He was standing in the open doorway looking so handsome in a white tuxedo, his locs pulled back in a ponytail. His roots were beginning to gray, but my daddy still looked big and young and handsome.

"I'm going to go take my place. See you two in a little bit," Aunt Kim said, leaving the room and closing the door behind her.

"You look so beautiful," my dad said, his voice quivering. "I can't believe my baby is really grown up and having her own baby. Where the fuck did the time go?"

I stood, pulling him into a hug as he wiped tears from his face. "No one can ever take your place. You're my daddy. You'll always be my daddy, and when I have this baby, she'll get to see what a wonderful father I was blessed to have in my life for all my life. Thank you for being my daddy."

"I'm honored to be your daddy. There are things in my life I wish I could go back and change but being your father will never be one of them. I'm hurt because a part of me wanted you to stay my little girl forever. I'm devastated because I didn't know On One was hurting you, but I'm confident you're in good hands now. That little nigga will fight a lion for you, just like I will."

I laughed into his chest. "Are you ever going to call him by his name?"

"Probably not."

He squeezed me tightly to him, cocooning me in his comfort and safety for a few minutes before walking me into my living room and presenting me to my handsome groom in his own white tuxedo, that diamond chain resting atop a white bow tie. I smiled. The only thought in my head?

Mine.

ARMAND

She had on this white dress that fit her so that you could see her round stomach. Wasn't no question that she was carrying my baby. That fact was obvious now. She was so beautiful that I found myself crying the second she stepped into the room. She was wearing makeup for the first time since the accident, and her hair was straight, falling past her shoulders. She was smiling. Her father was crying as hard as I was, but I don't think his tears were from joy.

It was her idea to get married at home and in private. It was also her idea to only invite a few people, family plus my best man, Scotty, and her guy of honor—some shit she made up—that Carlos nigga who I now believed was gay since he brought his dude with him. My little brothers and sister were excited to be there just like Ella's siblings were. It was a nice little crowd of folks, including all her uncles, who were mean-mugging me but hadn't threatened my life per Ella's request. Hell, even her Aunt Kat was giving me the eye.

Once she reached me, I took her hand and kissed it before we turned to face Mother Erica, who was evidently an ordained minister. She stood holding a sacred text and wearing a beautiful blue dress, a white cloth covering her hair.

"Sisters and brothers, kings and queens, we have assembled today for the joining of two tribes, the convergence of two nations...

As she spoke, more tears fell from my eyes. I was just...full. Full of love, full of happiness, full of disbelief that this was my life and this woman was about to be my wife. She was growing my baby inside her. Life was fucking unbelievable!

"...Armand and Ella have prepared their own vows. Armand," Mother Erica said, nodding at me.

We turned to face each other, hands joined. Sniffling, I began, "Ella, you've changed my life. You've helped me become a better man, a better *human.* You've taught me about patience and sacrifice. You're my paradise, my oasis, my shelter from everything that scares me. You're my dream come true. You're proof of what love can do. I love you. *I love you,* and I can't wait to spend the rest of my life showing you and our baby how much. I'm yours, *only yours*...forever."

Ella smiled at me as she lifted our joined hands to wipe tears from her face. "Armand, you've given me so much more than I could've asked for. You are my heartbeat, my sunshine, my happiness, my safe place, *my* dream come true. I love you so much, and I will love you in this life and the next. Thank you for being mine and only mine."

After we exchanged rings and our kiss had ended, I thought I would explode with pride when Mother Erica said, "I present to you all, with the blessings of the ancestors and in the love of Spirit, Mr. and Mrs. Armand DeShawn Daniels! Asé!"

Our witnesses enthusiastically agreed, "Asé!"

Well, everyone except for Ella's Uncle Lee Chester did. He very loudly yelled, "Ashtray!"

EPILOGUE

ARMAND

I'd assumed the position, my eyes on the rug, my arms behind my back and bound by rope as she circled me like a predator sizing up its prey, her now voluptuous body bare, a riding crop in her hand. When she stepped directly in front of me, I fixed my eyes on her feet, concentrating on the blue polish on her toenails.

"Look at me," she demanded.

I obeyed her, letting my eyes trail from her feet to her legs, over her thick thighs and soft stomach to her breasts, her *full* breasts. I stopped there, licking my lips at the sight of her glistening nipples.

"Look at my face, Armand. You're playing around knowing your daughter will wake up and put a stop to this."

My eyes snapped up to her beautiful face. "Sorry, sir."

Ignoring my apology, she grabbed a handful of my locs, jerking my head back and hyperextending my neck. Just as quickly as she'd grabbed my hair, she let it go, pressing her hairy mound to my face. I inhaled deeply.

Damn, she smelled good.

She backed away from me, and I closed my eyes. The next thing I felt was her untying the rope. When she squatted in front of me, I got a nose full of pussy, good, sweet, juicy pussy, and started drooling.

Lifting my chin with one hand, she kissed me deeply while playing with herself with the other. We kissed and she played for long minutes, then she grabbed my hand and placed it on her pussy. I groaned as I stroked her. She took her mouth from mine, throwing her head back while I licked and sucked on the warm flesh of her neck, alternating between stroking her clit and finger-fucking her until she began to howl my name.

Dropping her head, she stared at me for a moment before demanding, "Lie on your back so I can give you this pussy. You deserve it."

I stretched out on my back, lifting my head to see my dick disappear inside my wife, and enjoyed both the view and the ride.

I ROLLED over and reached for Ella only to find cold sheets. Sitting up, I turned the bedside lamp on and found her sitting in a chair we kept by the window in the bedroom. I loved watching my baby girl nurse.

"You brought her in here, sir?" I asked.

"Yeah, I wanted to watch you sleep while I fed her. You and Miami look just alike when you sleep, peaceful, but y'all love to raise hell when you're awake," Ella replied.

Miami McClain Daniels was only two months old, but Ella swore she looked like me. I saw more of Ella in her than me, from her brown eyes to her smooth skin. She was everything. Absolutely everything.

I grinned. "That's slander. I don't raise hell anymore unless I have to. Them stupid-ass On One fans better be glad they piped down because I was ready to wreck shop."

"Um, you just proved my point."

"You gon' stop slandering my baby, though. She don't be raising that much hell," I lied.

Ella smirked at me, and I chuckled before telling her, "You two look so beautiful right now. I'm sitting here tryna figure out how I got so lucky."

She smiled and looked down at Miami, rubbing her hand over her soft hair. "You're not the only one who got lucky."

Once Miami was finished eating, Ella took her back to her room, and when she returned to our bed, I pulled her to me and whispered in her ear, "I love you, sir."

"Hmmm," she hummed, snuggling closer to me, "I love you, too, Boogie."

ABOUT THE AUTHOR

A true southern girl, Alexandria House has an afinity for a good banana pudding, Neo Soul music, and tall black men in suits. When this music-loving fashionista is not shopping, she's writing steamy stories about real black love.

Connect with Alexandria!

Email: **msalexhouse@gmail.com**

Website: **http://www.msalexhouse.com/**

Newsletter: **http://eepurl.com/cOUVg5**

ALSO BY ALEXANDRIA HOUSE

ALSO BY ALEXANDRIA HOUSE

The Love After Series

Higher Love

Made to Love

Real Love

The Strickland Sisters Series

Stay with Me

Believe in Me

Be with Me

The McClain Brothers Series

Let Me Love You

Let Me Hold You

Let Me Show You

Let Me Free You

Let Me Please You (A McClain Family Novella)

The Them Boys Novella Series

Set

Jah

Shu

The Romey U Series

Teach Me

Touch Me

Temper Me

The St. Louis Cyclones Series

Flagrant

Technical

Personal

Short Works

Baby, Be Mine

Merry Christmas, Baby

Always My Baby

Should've Been

All I Want

New Year, New Boo?

Sanctuary (Paranormal)

the exhibition

Jingle Mingle

Short Story Collections

the love deluxe mixtape

the love galore mixtape

the love in!nite mixtape

The Holiday Shorts

Poetry